THE GHOST REALM

OGILVIE GRAY

ANDI CUMBO

THE PREFACE

Aloha! Hola! Annyeonghaseyo! Hi! Hello! Hullo! Hallo! Konichiwa! Blah blah blah! I am Ogilvie Gray. Bow before me in awe! Behold my superior awesomeness!

Okay. Now that we've gotten all the formalities out of the way, I would like to inform you of a few things:

1. Please, please, please keep some form of medical assistance at the ready in case of emergency. I don't want you choking to death on a hummus-dipped celery stick while you read one of the many hilarious parts of this book. That would be a terrible tragedy, and goodness knows we've had plenty of those in the long and well-documented history of the Homo sapiens.

2. If you are one of those people who hates romance with all their heart, dislikes it enough to want to encounter it as little as possible, or wants to avoid it at all costs, then you may find it wise to consider

skipping parts of pages 74 and 84, as those contain some romance. There is a bit of kissing in Part 2, but you should be fine, as there isn't much and it only appears occasionally.

3. Don't be eating a lot of snacks that are easy to spill, because this book is very precious and should be treated with the utmost care (except stroopwafels, however; they are perfectly fine for you to eat at all times).

I will stop boring you with these stupid instructions and warnings. I will now allow you to continue reading the actual story. So curl up next to your cozy fireplace (gas or wood-burning—doesn't matter); snuggle up in your favorite comforter; hug your elephant toy close to your heart; and prepare for a whole lot of laughter.

Signed,

One of the authors, Ogilvie Gray

PART ONE

CHAPTER
ONE

When it happened, I thought maybe a car had broken down at the end of our road and the boy had been sent to find help. He knocked on my door, and as I went to see who was there, the door swung open, and the boy walked in. He stood in the foyer and looked around at the dark wooden staircase, the iron chandelier, and the glass windows that opened onto the solarium, and then he said, "I'm hungry. Got anything to eat?"

I knew better than to be rude, so I took him into the kitchen, made him a ham and cheese sandwich, and poured him a glass of milk. I thought him a little impolite to ask if I had chocolate milk instead of plain milk, but it would have been very rude of me to point out his rudeness. So I just got the bottle of Hershey's out and squeezed some in.

After eating, he continued to sit at the kitchen island, so I finally decided I needed to know how I could help him and said, "Did you need something? Where are your parents?"

The boy tilted his head and looked at me. "I do think I need something, but I'm not sure what. I was asking myself that question when I showed up here."

I stared at him for a minute and willed him to answer my second query. Surely his parents—or parent, grandparent, or babysitter—were nearby. Our house wasn't exactly in town, and people didn't often wander up the half-mile lane and knock on our huge wooden door.

But the boy didn't say anything more. He just stared at the refrigerator like he was hungry again.

"Can I get you something else to eat? Are you still hungry?"

He shook his head. "No. Thanks, though. That's just the biggest refrigerator I've ever seen."

I turned to look at it and shrugged. It was big, I guess, but since it was the only refrigerator I'd ever seen, I didn't really have anything to compare it to.

I looked at the boy again, and he was spinning around on his stool to see the whole room. Then he stood up and walked toward the dumbwaiter in the corner. He pushed the button, and I heard the mechanics in the basement start up. A few moments later, the door opened, and a dish of chocolate ice cream with gummy bears was sitting in front of the boy.

"Whoa—I was just thinking that I wanted ice cream with gummy bears, and here it is." He spun to look at me. "That's amazing. How did you do that?"

"*I* didn't do it," I said to the boy, who was currently eyeing the dumbwaiter, no doubt thinking of all the sugary, unhealthy junk that could come out of the thing. "The dumbwaiter did." Then I rolled my eyes and walked closer to him. "Why are you here?"

"I—your house called to me," said the boy. He was surprisingly tall for his age, and he towered over me by at least a foot, as I was surprisingly short for my age (twelve). He looked

Hispanic—light brown skin, dark brown eyes—but his hair was surprising; it was a sandy-blond color, styled in a buzz cut.

"The house called to you?!" I repeated. I had heard many, many odd things in my time (once, Dad had used the word "cupcakes" as a curse word when he'd accidentally dropped a hammer on his big toe), and I lived in a house with a magical dumbwaiter. But what this boy was saying probably topped them all. "I'm sorry, but that is the exact opposite of believable."

"I know," the boy said. "I know it sounds crazy."

Oh, you bet *it sounds crazy,* I thought to myself.

"Look," I said to the boy, "you can't stay here."

"Why not?" he asked.

"Because you literally just barged into my home, and I have no idea who you are. How do I know that you're not here to kidnap me or kill me or both?" I took a deep breath, as I had just said all this all at once. "And," I added, "won't your parents be worried?"

"My parents won't be worried. They died a few years ago. Car crash." He looked a little sad as he said this. Well, actually, he looked very, very sad, but he looked like he was trying to (unsuccessfully) hide the fact that he was sad. "And you're right. I shouldn't have invaded your privacy like that. I'm sorry."

"It's okay," I said. If the boy *did* try to kidnap me or worse, I had a handy selection of heavy cast-iron pans in the kitchen. "But about your parents? God, I'm so sorry . . . whoever you are."

"Paco," he said. "Paco Solberg."

"Solberg," I repeated. "Isn't that a Norwegian surname?"

"Yeah," said Paco. "I'm Mexican-Norwegian."

Ah-*ha!* So *that* was why his hair color was so weird.

"Well, Paco Solberg," I said, "lovely to make your acquaintance. I'm Cassidy Weldon."

CHAPTER

TWO

I left my odd new sort-of friend in the family room and ran upstairs. The staff was all off since it was Sunday, so the house was basically all mine for the day. I would let Paco stay for the day and then send him back home.

I went into my room, which had posters of the Rolling Stones, Nirvana, Metallica, AC/DC, and various other bands pasted to the walls. Clothing was thrown across the floor. My bedsheets and blankets had been tossed on the ground as well. I entered the bathroom, which was pretty much the only clean space in my room (only because one of my caretakers had insisted that I clean it, even though I didn't want to). I headed straight for the mirror.

My hair's original color was a very, very dark brown, but a few months ago, I had dyed it a rich, vibrant electric green. Since then, the color had faded to more of a lime-green color, plus my hair had grown, so my roots were their natural hue. My hair had not responded well to the bleach and the dye—I had horrible split ends (seriously, I once counted exactly twenty-two splits on a single strand), and my hair stuck out in some places. It was very long—about midway down my back —and took at least half an hour to brush if it was one of its (rare) good days. My hair was an absolute nightmare to deal with, but I didn't look good in any other hairstyle.

One of my favorite facial features was my nose. It was a very nice nose. Long and straight, it had a slightly pointed end. It was one of my only good features. Another favorite was my high cheekbones. People said that I'd inherited them from Dear Ol' Dad, but the thing is, *both* of my parents had high cheekbones (weird). And as for my eyes, I tended to use so much eyeshadow and mascara that it smeared and made it look like I had not slept properly in a month. I didn't like my eye color, which was a bluish-gray, because it clashed with my green hair.

I reached for a hair tie and pulled my hair back in a ponytail. Then I headed back downstairs.

When I entered the living room, Paco looked up, halfway through what looked like his fourth gummy bear ice cream sundae. He had a chocolate ice cream mustache, and his words sounded all garbled together when he spoke around a large spoonful of ice cream. "Hey, you're back."

"Duh," I said. I sat next to him on the couch. "Now that I've returned, you are going to explain to me in great detail— without leaving *anything* out, anything, ya hear?—why the heck you're here."

Paco shoved another huge spoonful into his mouth, chewing on the gummy bears with what could only be described as pure, absolute bliss. I wasn't sure if he had heard me, but then he spoke. "Okay, okay, I will." With one last mouthful, he set the cup aside and shifted his position.

I noted with approval that he had taken off his shoes before putting his feet on the couch.

Paco cleared his throat and began to speak. "Okay, so it's

Friday. I'm in the library, organizing books on the shelves 'cause I work at the library. Then I come across this ancient-looking book that has, like, a ton of dust on it. I swear, it's like no one's touched it for a century or something. And so after sneezing for like ten minutes straight—I'm allergic to dust mites—I grab a towel and wipe off the cover. Honestly, it looks more like a journal than a book. Anyway. So I open the thing. It's a collection of local legends. And I come across one of the stories, and it's about this huge mansion and a whole family that disappears."

"Creepy," I said.

Paco talked fast, without taking a breath for the entire speech, and I was a little overwhelmed.

I'd have to buy a pair of earplugs next time my babysitter took me shopping. "Go on."

"So I finish the book and put it back where it belongs," said Paco, "which is in the fiction section, in case you're wondering."

I wasn't.

"And suddenly—and I know this sounds super, super weird—there's this voice inside my head. It was all deep and thunderous and important-sounding and everything. Ya wanna know what it said?"

"Paco," I said, "I just told you to tell me everything."

"Right, right. Sorry. Well, it said, 'Yo, Pac-Man. What up, dude?' I helloed it back, and it said, 'I am the Spirit of the House on the Half-Mile Lane, a bus ride from here. You can call me Alfred, but if you like, you have my permission to address me as Alfie. Now that we've exchanged greetings and name preferences, let's get on with the important stuff.' So I wait to hear what it says next. 'Pac-Man, there is something I must tell you.' Suspenseful pause. 'Pac-Man, do you know where McDonald's is?' I said to him, 'Of course I do. I go there every

Friday night for dinner with my abuelita.' He says, 'Oh, you do? Excellent, then. Adjacent to McDonald's, Pac-Man, is a fork in the road that is simply called "The Fork." Notice how I rolled the R in "Fork." Choose the left side of The Fork, not the right one. Never the right one. On the left side of The Fork, there is a lane. Keep going until you reach the sixth house on the lane. That house, Pac-Man, is My House. The House. Notice how I said "The House" with an Austrian accent. There, a girl lives. Say hello to the girl.' 'Then what?' I asked. No answer. Alfie left my mind."

"So you just followed the voice's instructions?" I asked. "Paco, that voice . . . Alfred . . . Alfie . . . Whatever the heck you call it, that voice was obviously a figment of your overactive imagination. Have you been sleeping well?"

"I've been sleeping fine," said Paco. "And anyway, I did what you told me—*cough,* ordered me—to, *cough.* I gave you the truth and the whole truth. Cross my heart and hope to die, stab a chunk of obsidian in my eye."

"That sounds very painful," I said. "Please do not do that."

"And besides," he went on, "that sort of thing is not my imagination. Do you actually think I would ever make up something like that?"

"Actually," I said, "I do."

Paco ignored me. "Alfie was who I was talking about when I told you that the house called to me."

"Well, how was I supposed to know that?" I asked indignantly.

Paco shrugged. "Dunno." And with that, the boy went back to his ice cream.

I sat back and stared at the wall in front of me for a minute. The big cup of Pepsi I'd spilled last week had left little droplets all over the wall, and I'd kept meaning to clean them up. They bugged me, and it bugged me, too, that the housekeeper hadn't even seen them yet. Did I have to do everything around here?

With a huff, I got up to go to the cleaning closet and get a rag and some spray. I knew I was grumpy because I didn't quite understand what Paco was telling me about my own home, but it was easier to be mad at the wall and the housekeeper than at Paco and his chocolate face or even my own house.

As I wiped away droplets of sticky soda, I vacillated between thinking Paco might need professional mental health care and being surprisingly upset by the possibility that my house had called to him.

I loved my house. It was bright and sunny, and it had a billion nooks and crannies where I could sit and read or listen to music. It smelled just like home was supposed to smell—a little dusty, a little bit like vanilla, and a lot like whatever the cook was making for dinner. Plus, it was the only place where I felt I could really be myself.

So why hadn't the house ever told *me* it had a name?

Clearly, my brain and emotions were landing me on the side of believing Paco, but I didn't necessarily want to believe him, because if I did, I would have to contend with a lot. First, a strange boy was eating copious amounts of ice cream in my living room because he had been summoned here. Second, my house was summoning people without consulting me. Third, my house had a name and, apparently, a kind of quirky personality and had not as of yet revealed any of that to me.

But there didn't seem to be any way to convince myself that Paco was mentally unwell, no matter how hard I tried, and that realization made me wonder why that was.

"It's because you know me, Cassidy," a voice somehow both inside and outside of myself said.

I resisted the urge to spin around and look for the voice like people always do in books and movies. Instead, I stood stock-still and looked at my shoes, brown penny loafers with actual pennies in them because I appreciated the retro look they gave my feet.

For a second, I thought about replying to the voice, but I knew if I did, I'd have to rope myself into the same corral as I'd put Paco in. I wasn't ready to do that yet.

"Believing in magic doesn't make you crazy, Cassidy," the voice said. "In fact, it maybe makes you one of the last well people in the world."

I really liked the voice's line of thinking, but at twelve, I had long been indoctrinated in the teachings of the world that said magic wasn't real. Everything from Santa to fairies to phoenixes to angels was a myth created to explain something that was as of yet unexplainable to some people. My mom had taught me that a long time ago, and I needed to believe her.

I really needed to believe her, or else my house was talking.

"I would never be one to contradict your mother, Cassidy, but all people are wrong sometimes." The voice sounded kind, understanding even. It also sounded like an adult, and it had been a very long time since an adult had really talked to me about something other than what I needed to physically survive. I didn't realize until that moment that I was missing the care of an adult person.

Was this voice a person? A figment? A figment of a person? Gracious, I was confusing myself.

"Um," I said. "Are you Alfred?" It made me feel very weird to be talking to a wall.

"Goodness, no!" said the voice. "Alfie decided to take some time off today. I'm just substituting for him."

"Are you a house spirit too?" I asked.

"One of the last, sadly. Humans don't seem to need us as much as they used to. I'm Sally."

"I'm Cassidy."

"I know that. Alfie is always babbling on and on about you. You seem to be his favorite person," Sally said.

Now I was even more confused. "Favorite person? But I've never even met him."

"True, true," said Sally. "But he's been watching over you ever since you came into this world twelve years ago. He's rather enjoying seeing you grow up."

"Why would he tell Paco about me and the house and not tell me?" I asked. Realizing she didn't know who Paco was, I added, "Paco's the guy in the family room, stuffing his face with ice cream."

"I don't know, dear," Sally said kindly, "but I do know that Alfie knows what he's doing."

"I hope so," I said.

Sally didn't answer.

I tried calling out to her again for a bit, gave up, and went back to cleaning. House spirits seemed to have a bad habit of shutting off at totally random times.

I decided that I was probably hallucinating, finished wiping up the Pepsi spill, threw away the now-brown rag, and went to take my medicine, which I'd forgotten to take, as Paco had been occupying all of my attention.

I passed the family room on the way to my room. Paco wasn't there—probably playing with the dumbwaiter again. I climbed up the stairs, avoided piles of dirty clothing as I navigated the messiness of my room, got to the bathroom, and took out my medicine from the medicine cabinet.

"What's that?" a familiar voice asked.

I jumped about a foot in the air. "Paco?!"

"Yup. 'Tis me," he said. He leaned against the doorframe.

"What did I say about snooping around?!" I roared.

"Nothing, actually."

Oh, right. I made a mental note to devise a list of rules for

Paco to follow in my house, which was not going to be long since he was just so annoying.

"Well, from now on," I said, "snooping around in my home is prohibited."

"Noted," he said. He pointed at the small container of pills in my hand and asked again, "What's that?"

"Medicine."

"For what?"

I really didn't want him to know, so I made up a lie. "Um, well. I've got . . . the flu. Yeah, the flu."

"The flu?" Paco said. One of his blond eyebrows was slightly higher than the other, giving him a permanently skeptical look, but I could tell from his voice that he was actually suspicious.

"Yeah. A really, really bad case."

He raised his eyebrow even higher. "Why, Cassidy, I do believe that you're not being entirely truthful with me."

"Fine," I said. "You really want to know?" I was a terrible liar, and I kind of thought it might be nice to tell someone my age.

He nodded.

I sighed. "I have a spontaneous incurable disease that I will probably die from before I reach twenty. It has no name, and it's a completely new illness that no one else in the world has. It baffles the doctors and befuddles the nurses. My disease affects my mind, so I have to take these pills twice daily to help slow the process of gradually spiraling into madness. The doctors aren't sure, but they think that—hopefully many, many years from now—the disease will just cause my brain to stop working and then I will be dead. End of story."

"Okay, that wasn't what I was expecting," said Paco.

"What were you expecting, then?" I asked.

He shrugged. "Dunno."

"You can go away now," I told him.

Thankfully, he did. He left my room, and a minute later, I heard the front door slam shut.

I popped the pills in my mouth and swallowed them, making a sour face. They tasted horrible. But at least they worked.

I went downstairs, threw away the empty cups of ice cream that Paco had left on the couch, and sat down to watch *Stranger Things*.

CHAPTER
THREE

Dearest Cassidy,

How are you doing? We hope you're well. We have been having a simply wonderful time. Dad has made a brand-new friend whose name is Josh. Josh is very handsome, has a passion for cauliflower and mushroom harvesting, and enjoys bodysurfing on the beach. The Bahamas are quite lovely. All sunshine all year round. The perfect place to get a tan.

Dad has lost quite a bit of weight thanks to his new vegan diet, and guess what? Your mom is pregnant! We're coming home in a week for your birthday and staying for two days. Expect to have vegan meals.

Love, Mother and Father

I crumpled up the letter and tossed it into the trash can, but not before drawing little red horns and tails in permanent marker on a picture of my parents that had been included in the envelope.

My parents were huge narcissists, and thanks to the money earned from being famous actors, they could do basically whatever their greedy little self-absorbed hearts desired. This included going on year-long vacations to expensive places, abandoning their daughter at home and hiring tutors and babysitters to take care of her. Mom had been practicing the art of sunbathing for so long now that her skin was quite literally a shade of darkish brown. She'd also bleached her hair blond. Back when she had been a normal mother, which had been up to when I'd turned eight, her handwriting had looked like this:

DEAR CASSIDY

BUT NOW HER handwriting was evenly-spaced and loopy, and her letters were all written in bright fuchsia ink. Back when she'd been a normal mother, she would slap enormous piles of sunscreen on me, Dad, and herself whenever we went outside for long periods of time. She had been the coolest mom ever—until I turned eight. Dad nowadays was a bald, sunburnt guy with a potbelly and had a particular interest in gaudy paisley shirts and golf. Before I was eight, he had had a head full of thin salt-and-pepper hair, hated golf (he'd insisted it was far too boring), and worked out at the local gym every day.

Yup, my parents had definitely changed. I suspected that this was all because of my disease. I'd been seven years old when, one night, I thought that my favorite doll, whom I called

Rose, was talking to me. The next morning, I had babbled about my "conversation" with Rose over breakfast. This continued until I was eight, when my parents, out of concern for my health, had finally taken me to the doctor. And thus my disease was diagnosed at last. I guess the stress of having a daughter with mental health issues was too much for them, and they just left.

Now, some of the only times my parents visited me were at Christmas, my birthday, and Hanukkah, because my governor, Mr. Watts, was Jewish.

I strolled into the family room, where Mr. Watts was lounging on one of the beanbag chairs. "Mom and Dad are coming home next week for my birthday."

"Your birthday? Goodness, child. I didn't realize it was December already!" said Mr. Watts. "Ah, how the time flies, eh?"

I smiled. No matter how depressed my parents made me, Mr. Watts could always cheer me up. He used to be an amateur comedian based in Toronto, so he would crack jokes at random intervals. Mr. Watts had shaggy blond hair, blue eyes, a crooked grin, a mustache, a Polish accent, and owned an incredibly large collection of top hats. I counted myself lucky that I had a caretaker like him.

"We should start planning for the party!" Mr. Watts decided. "Only a week, and so much to get done. What do you want for your birthday?"

"Parents who act like parents," I said.

He laughed. "Good one! Hey, maybe we should play a prank on them."

"Maybe. Not on my dad, though. He'll probably be really cranky because he just turned vegan, and now bacon is off-limits to him," I said, and then corrected myself: "Well, crankier than usual."

Mr. Watts nodded seriously. "Good point. But we can still pull on your mother, yes?"

"Yeah, all she'll give us is a quick scolding."

Giggling hilariously, we began plotting our revenge against my mom and dad, pausing only to snarf down some ginger-snap cookies.

Many, many cookies and revenge-plotting sessions later . . .

MR. WATTS and I had just finished putting our final touches on our Ultimate Prank when the doorbell rang three times, which I knew was my mother's way of saying, "Hi, I'm here!" The doorbell had stopped properly functioning about a year ago, so instead of emitting a pleasant *ding-dong*, it squeaked horribly. My other guardian, a young woman named Chelsea, intended to buy a new one, but with all of the other chores there was to do, it kept slipping people's minds. I didn't really care, though. As long as it annoyed the heck out of my parents, that doorbell was fine with me.

I raced for the door and opened it. I put on my best fake-happy face, which wasn't super great, and greeted my parents. "Hi, Mom and Dad, Dad and Mom!"

"Don't forget the baby," said Mom, patting her swollen tummy.

I rolled my eyes. "Right. Can't forget the newest addition to our *very messed up family!* Hi, unborn baby."

"That's the spirit!" Mom beamed.

Dad just grunted. Dad grunted all the time.

"Now, do let us in, will you?"

"Certainly!" This time, my grin was not false. In fact, it

could be described as slightly, if not extremely, maniacal. Everything was going according to plan.

I swung the door open wider and beckoned them inside. "Please, come in!"

Mom stepped forward, and immediately, her foot caught on a piece of thin dental floss, which was tied to the handle of a huge full-to-the-brim watering can, which was attached to several fake but surprisingly realistic spiders that we normally used for Halloween. The watering can fell over and started raining on her, and the spiders dangled around her head.

Mom screeched in terror, while Dad stood on the doorstep, having not moved an inch. She was deathly afraid of spiders and hated being sprayed with water. It was the perfect prank.

When the water finally ran out, and once she'd realized that the spiders were in fact fake, Mom calmed down a bit. Her beehive hairdo was in disarray, and her makeup needed touching up.

I lay on the floor, laughing so hard that everything hurt. This was even better than I'd hoped for. Watching from the banister, Mr. Watts gave me a grin and a double thumbs-up.

Mom, however, was not smiling. She wasn't freaking out anymore, but she was livid—with me specifically. "Cassidy Weldon, go to your room," she said with a calm that was far scarier than shouting.

I looked up at her from the floor and actually started to laugh harder. Who did she think she was? My mother? To actually be my mother she'd have to act like one all the time, not just when she was mad.

With a little help from Chelsea, I got up off the floor and began to clean up the remains of the prank. I hated a mess. While I wound the floss and gathered the spiders, I tried to control my laughter, more from worry about the innocent baby inside my mother than from any concern for her, but I couldn't stop thinking about how successful Operation Frank, the name Mr. Watts and I had given our plan, had been. The rhyming made us both giggle.

I glanced up at the top of the staircase, where Mr. Watts had surreptitiously placed himself when he heard the doorbell ring, and saw that he was shaking with laughter. He, however, had the sense not to let my mother see.

Instead, Mom was entirely focused on me, which—despite the fact that I did wish she was around more—was actually never a good thing. Her attention was never kind, and today was no exception. "What have you done to your hair, young woman? And is that eyeshadow? Who gave you permission to wear eyeshadow?"

I braced myself for what I knew was coming next, an attempted banishment to my bathroom to wash my face and fix my hair.

"No one," I said truthfully. I had just started wearing eyeshadow a year ago, and nobody had stopped me, so I figured it would be fine.

Mom pointed a sharp, extremely long red fingernail in the direction of my room. "We are not happy about this, Cassidy. We will have a little chit-chat after our vegan, sugar-free dinner, got that? Now, go wash off that horrid stuff. You look simply frightful."

"Fine, fine, I will," I said. So I went upstairs, washed off my black-eye makeup (which was, in my opinion, kind of cool because I looked like a zombie) and put on some death metal (which I didn't really like, but I knew that my parents would hate it), purposely turning the volume up as loud as possible to further aggravate my parents. My ears hurt horribly from the volume and the squealing of the electric guitars, and I was sure my eardrums were just about ready to burst.

I faintly heard my dad screaming from downstairs, "Cut that %@#$&* music out!"

I was enjoying this greatly.

Just as the song ended (giving my poor ears a break for a few beautiful seconds), my phone rang. I didn't recognize who was calling, but something in my gut told me to pick up. I picked it up.

"Hello?" I said into the phone.

"Cassidy? Hi, Cassidy!"

Oh, dear. Oh, no. It was Paco. "Paco? How do you know my phone number?" I demanded.

"Oh, I was just fooling around, making prank calls. I don't have a lot to do these days," he said casually.

"Okay, well, bye," I said.

"Bye. But now you know my number, so you can call me if you need to."

"Okay. As if I'll ever need it," I said.

"Hey, you never know," Paco said. "Anyway, I should go now. I gotta go meet my abuelita at McDonald's."

"Bye," I said again. There was a click, and my music started playing, the singer shrieking something about love at the top of his lungs.

"CASSIDY!" Dad yelled. "Stop that horrible music! Also, it's dinnertime."

"FINE!" I hollered back. I paused the song like a good, obedient daughter, tramped downstairs like a good, obedient daughter, and sat at the kitchen table like a good, obedient daughter. I sat next to Chelsea, which was the seat farthest away from my parents.

"Cassidy," said Mom, "we would first like to thank you for stopping that terrible, squealy sound. You have saved your mother from a massive headache."

"Uh-huh. You're so not welcome," I said. It must be noted

that my mother had a horrible habit of speaking in the third person. I couldn't remember the last time she'd uttered the word "I."

"Language, young lady," Dad cautioned, then grunted. Whenever he *did* speak, it usually had a cuss word or two in it. So frankly, *he* should've been the one minding his language, but I digress. Dads will be dads.

Just then our cook, Frances, whirled into the room, her colorful skirts swishing about her ankles gracefully. She held several platters of Mystery Something, masterfully balancing one on her head and the other two in her arms. She set them down on the table, cleared her throat, straightened her blond hair, smoothed the creases in her shirt, and announced in her Texas accent, "Your dinner, ladies and gentlemen."

"Exquisite," said Mom. "What are the dishes?"

"Vegan sugar-free dressing-less salad, sugar-free pad Thai with tofu, and apples dipped in mayonnaise," said Frances. "I do hope it's to your satisfaction."

"Oh, we're sure it will be just wonderful, right, honey-buns?" Mom said to Dad.

Dad grunted.

And so the meal began, the grown-ups all making polite conversation, though their hearts were not exactly in it. I was mostly ignored, though Mr. Watts showed me a card trick and talked about The Ultimate Prank.

Dinner ended pretty much the same way that it started, with poor Frances asking if everything was good, Mom assuring her that everything was delicious (which it actually was), and Dad grunting along. Then we ended with sugar-free popsicles for dessert.

After the staff had left the table, I received a long lecture about responsibility and how pulling a prank on Mother Dearest was not at all nice. As far as punishments go, it was actually the worst of Mom and Dad's arsenal. They didn't believe in time-out or sending children to their room, and they would certainly never have grounded me. That was demeaning to my humanity. Instead, they chose lectures, and those were definitely a punishment. I usually glazed over at some point and thought about anything else: how many petals were on the usual rose, what color eye shadow I would torture them with next—that kind of thing. Then I was sent off to bed with an intensity that made me think my parents considered that the actual punishment, when in actuality, it was just nice to get away.

In my room, I turned on some white noise and fell asleep, my dreams consisting of Paco sharing barbecue with a neon-pink penguin dressed in a tuxedo who spoke with an Australian accent, with rowdy music blasting out of a speaker. It was the most restful sleep I'd had in a long while.

The next morning I woke up late, got up, dressed, got breakfast, grabbed my library card, borrowed Mr. Watts's credit card, threw on several warm coats, put on earmuffs, and stepped outside, my faded green hair swirling in the fierce wind. My breath came out as steam, floating almost magically away with the breeze. It hadn't snowed yet, because it rarely snows around Christmastime where I live, but it was absolutely frigid. Even with several layers of very warm clothing—I'd even put on the horrible woolen turtleneck sweater my Aunt Lucy had made for me a couple years ago—I shivered.

My parents were away today, probably partying somewhere at a fancy-schmancy salon or something, so I was basically free. And because Chelsea and Mr. Watts knew how depressed my parents made me, they let me go wild. I realized that I had not thanked them for this unnecessary kindness, and I made a mental note to make them a nice card later.

I strolled down my lane, came to The Fork, and stared at

the right side for a moment. I'd never been down that way, because there was nothing but a dead end and the beginnings of a huge forest. At least that's what GPS said.

I kept walking on the small trail that continued at the end of the actual road, and because this was a fairly small town, I arrived at the local library in less than fifteen minutes.

I flung open the huge double doors, and a blast of warm air greeted me. I smelled the wonderful aroma of books, books, books, new and old, classic and unclassic. I loved the library. It's where I got most of my education because I homeschooled myself with a little guidance from the tutors who were actually supposed to do the work. The library was also a lovely place with a large mural on the ceiling depicting scenes from the Bible, the Thomas Jefferson quote "I cannot live without books" written in loopy letters across one of the walls, several post-Stone Age computers with really good Internet service, friendly librarians, and—best of all—about a million gazillion shelves full of nothing but books. Paradise.

I waved to the librarians as I passed by the front desk, and they waved back. I immediately went to the fiction section and scanned the shelves. Eventually, I spotted the book Paco had been rambling on and on about (really, it wasn't that hard to find; most of the tomes around it were brand-new with shiny, glossy covers), pulled it down from the shelf, and dove in.

I read the whole thing in about thirty minutes, pausing only to drink some water from the water fountain near the bathroom. The book was actually kind of interesting, though some of the language used was a bit hard to understand with terms and references I just didn't know. I read through the story about the missing family, but no thunderous voice rang throughout my head; I had expected that, but some part of me was still a tiny bit disappointed.

I decided to check out this book to investigate it further

because my Nancy Drew-sense was kicking in, and then I picked out a novel that seemed rather interesting—something about flying gargoyles and pencil eaters or such.

As I rounded the corner of the shelf, figuring out how to escape from this maze of bookshelves (even after years of visiting the library, I still got lost), I bumped into a someone with dreadlocks and dark brown skin. Books went flying, and a few curses were uttered on my part. I quickly got up and offered a hand to the unfortunate individual with whom I had just collided. "Are you okay?"

"Yeah, I'm good. Thanks," the person said, standing up. A pin on their shirt read "THEY/THEM." They rubbed their head, wincing slightly. "Got conked on the noggin pretty good, but I think I'll survive."

"Well, that's good news," I said, relieved. "What's your name?"

"X," they said. "Just X."

"I'm Cassidy."

X smiled and handed my books back to me. "Here. You dropped these."

I accepted them with a grateful smile. "Thank you. You dropped these, too." I picked their books up and gave them back to them.

"Thanks again," said X, tucking them under their arm. They nodded toward one of the books I was holding. "I've read that one. It's pretty good."

"I hope so," I told them. "Nice to meet you, X."

"Back at ya," they said, and we headed in separate directions.

I went my usual way back home to my house and set myself up in my ideal reading situation—a glass of milk, a glass of seltzer water, a plate of whatever mildly unhealthy thing I could find (today's choice was olive hummus and crackers), and a candle. None of that scented stuff. No, I preferred a single white taper. I felt like Edgar Allan Poe when I lit it.

With a quick scan of the room to be sure no ravens were perched on the bookshelves of the living room, I turned to my new books from the library. It was only then that I discovered I didn't have Paco's mystery book anymore. Instead, I was looking at a Guinness Book of World Records from 1938. A fascinating choice, for sure, but not exactly what I had been expecting to study.

I realized I must have accidentally swapped books with X. I didn't panic, though, because I had learned a long time ago that I couldn't control most things in the world, and since I had no idea how to find X short of being that creepy kid trying to get someone else's address or phone number from the librarian, I decided to just wait and see what would happen.

Meanwhile, I spent a couple of hours learning what world records I might achieve without a single skill except not performing any personal hygiene. I knew I couldn't do the fingernail thing—too gross. And I was fairly certain I couldn't stand to let my hair grow long. But eyeball popping? That might be an option. I'd just have to practice.

My route to fame chosen, I spent the rest of the afternoon reading my novel and pushing my eyes forward as part of the preliminary stage of my training. By the time my parents got home, just before another delightful, vegan sugar-free dinner, my eye sockets ached, but I had achieved at least a millimeter of pop. I was on my way to fame and not so much fortune.

I went back to the library the next day, hoping to find X to give them their book back. After much exploring of the maze of heaven called the library, I finally located them at one of the library's computers, looking up Andrew Carnegie on Wikipedia. I cleared my throat to notify them of my presence, and they turned around in their swivel chair, startled to see me.

"Cassidy!" they said. "Didn't see you there."

"Sorry if I'm bothering you," I said meekly, "but yesterday, I realized we accidentally swapped books. I was hoping to find you so I could return it to you."

"I did, too," said X, absent-mindedly running a hand through their dreadlocks. They smiled at me, their white teeth sharply contrasting against their cocoa-dark skin. "That was really thoughtful, trying to find me to give it back. Matter of fact, I was thinkin' of doing the same. I brought your book with me." They reached into their bright-orange backpack, which was sitting on the floor beside their chair, and withdrew Paco's book. They gave it to me, and I gave their World Records book back to them.

X tapped the cover of my book. "Read this last night. Did some quick research on ghosts, found some cool stuff you might like to know."

"Why?" I asked, curious.

X shrugged. "Dunno, you just kinda strike me as the kind of gal who likes ghost stuff."

"Why would you assume that?" I demanded, even though he was right.

X shrugged again. "I dunno. Guess it's 'cause of the green hair."

I grinned. "Maybe."

"So if you ever planning on summoning a ghost," said X, smiling, "turn off all of the lights in your house, and light a candle or somethin'. Ghosts are attracted to light, so a single flickering light in the dark will get their attention. Also, for some crazy reason, they love Sprite. So make sure to have a coupla cans of that around."

"Well, that's interesting," I said.

"Yeah," they agreed, "it is."

I talked with X a bit longer about their research finds,

mostly because I was curious about what in the book had led them to be so interested in ghosts, but also, I had to admit, because I was beginning to wonder whether I might need some of that information at my house. I wasn't sure how I felt about that possibility.

After a few minutes, I said goodbye to them and exited the library. It was mid-morning, but I hadn't eaten breakfast yet, so I was starving. There was a bakery right across the street, conveniently, so I crossed and entered the bakery.

The bakery was actually more like a cafe than just a bakery counter. It smelled like coffee and had several couches and recliners for people to sit on, with the Wi-Fi password scrawled on a whiteboard that rested on one of the many tables. I dug a wad of cash out of my pocket, ordered a large hot chocolate, a blueberry muffin, a buttery croissant (because I just can't resist French food), and a chunk of yummy-looking fudge. Not the healthiest breakfast—Mom would be shocked at the amount of sugar I was consuming—but most of the stuff the bakery served had a lot of sugar in it, so I didn't really have a choice. Also, I was craving sugary stuff.

After I received my food, I sat down on the nearest couch and stuffed my face. Minutes passed before I finally looked up from my plate and realized there was another person at the table. A person I happened to recognize with a feeling of dread. A person with short, sand-colored hair, considerable height, light brown skin, and a backwards Yankees baseball cap.

Oh, dear.

Paco.

"Paco?" I mumbled around a mouthful of fudge.

"I was wondering when you'd notice me." Paco checked his Apple watch. "It took you exactly ten minutes and fifty seconds before you realized I was here."

I reddened. "I was hungry, okay?"

"I could tell." Paco leaned back. "Please, continue eating. I don't want to ruin your fudge."

"Too late," I said. I chewed, swallowed, wiped my mouth with a napkin, and said, "You told me you worked at the library, and yet I haven't seen you there."

"Oh, that's because you always come at the wrong times," he told me. "This is my morning break, which lasts half an hour. I don't work full-time, either. I only work on Wednesdays and Fridays."

"Oh," I said. This made sense.

I finished eating and fished the strange book out of my bag. "Recognize this?"

"Oh, yeah, there's no way I wouldn't recognize that," Paco said, chuckling. "It's literally falling apart. The spine needs to be fixed, and the leather of the cover is cracked."

"Right. I've looked through it about eleven times already, and I have heard no strange voices in my head giving me directions to my house."

"So?" Paco took a sip of coffee.

"So this proves that you need to see a doctor!" I said.

"Why?"

Good grief, was he really this dumb? Annoyed, I said, "Because you 'heard' a voice in your head that led you to my house!"

This time he understood. "I don't think this proves that I have mental health issues. In fact, you yourself told me that you have a disease that affects your mental health, so you could be the one who is imagining this all."

"Maybe," I said. I put the book away and rose to leave. "Well, bye." And I walked out, leaving him alone.

For the second time that day, a new friend had said things that I didn't really want to deal with. I really needed some new friends who would lie to me, maybe.

CHAPTER

FOUR

For the next few days, nothing strange happened. Christmas was in exactly a week, and everyone (except my parents) was rushing to decorate the house for the holiday. We brought our old fake-but-surprisingly-realistic tree out from the basement and had fun putting the ornaments on. Mr. Watts hoisted me up on his shoulders and let me put the star on the tree while Mom loudly threatened to sue him if he dropped me.

Ah, yes, your typical Weldon family holiday gathering.

It turned out that Mom was due to give birth to the baby right before Christmas, which was kind of exciting. I wanted to have a baby sibling and hoped that they would not turn out the same way as my parents—selfish, self-absorbed, and completely narcissistic. I also secretly wanted to be given the important task of naming the baby. I couldn't decide between Eva or Ada, so I compromised between the two—Eda.

It was on my thirteenth birthday, December 21, when everything changed.

The sky had decided to gift me with heavy snow for my birthday, so when I looked out of the window after I woke up, the ground was covered in several inches. I gazed toward the sky, thanked it for its wonderful present (I loved snow), hopped out of bed, and went downstairs, still in my old Berenstain Bears jammies (for some reason, they still fit me, which was astonishing). I loved those things. They were so soft and warm.

Mom was still in bed—probably getting her oh-so-important beauty rest—but I could smell bacon sizzling in the kitchen. We hadn't eaten any meat in weeks, so this could only mean one thing: Dad was violating his diet. Hoo, boy. Mom would be upset. I could already hear her shrill screams of outrage in my mind.

I raced to the kitchen, and sure enough, Dad was cooking bacon in a pan, with poor Frances cowering behind him.

"Mr. Weldon, sir, please! Mrs. Weldon will be furious!" Frances begged.

"I don't care if she's angry or not!" Dad bellowed at the top of his lungs, which was sure to wake everyone up. "I hate this @#@^#^$^ diet! I WANT MEAT!"

"Hi, Frances. Hi, Dad," I said. "Frances is right, Dad. Mom might not be too happy with your decision to go back to being a total carnivore."

"DON'T CARE!" Dad hollered. "Must! Eat! Now!"

"Okay, okay," I said. "Like I always say, do what ya gotta do."

Frances gave me a platter of cookies and a steaming hot chocolate. "Here you go, darlin'."

"Thanks, Frances!" I said. I picked up one of the cookies and took a bite, the chocolate chips melting in my mouth. "Mmmm!"

"You probably should go outside," Frances told me. "Things are bound to get ugly in a moment."

"You're right," I agreed, confident that my plate of cookies would do nothing to improve my mother's mood. I hugged Frances, tossed on the heaviest coat I could find, and went onto the back patio, which was fortunately covered, so I was shielded from the snow.

A minute later, Frances's prediction turned out to be correct.

A horrified, slightly muffled scream came from the kitchen, followed by my mother swearing in French and then yelling at Dad, "YOU JUST GOT THIN AGAIN!"

The birds—mostly crows—rose from the treetops in panicked flocks at the sound of her vociferous, high-pitched voice. I giggled to myself quietly as I ate, listening to Mom shrieking French curse words and throwing plates and wine glasses in her tantrum.

Eventually, this ended, and I was able to go back inside. I helped Frances and the other staff clean up the mess made by Mom's whirlwind of destruction, then took a soda from the fridge and went to my room. I had added a couple more Nirvana posters to my wall, and I had cleaned up a bit due to my Mom's orders. She couldn't abide any kind of mess, even though I had never—literally never—seen her clean anything herself.

I sat on my bed, which smelled inexplicably of lavender even though Chelsea was allergic to the stuff. I sipped my soda and read one of my many books while The Rolling Stones played from my little portable speaker. And then it happened: Alfie spoke to me at last.

"Hello," a deep, thunderous voice with just a hint of an Italian accent said.

I jumped so high I swear my head brushed the ceiling, then fell back onto my bed, bouncing a couple of times. "What the heck!"

"Oh, did I startle you? I'm so sorry; that was quite rude of me. I do hope you'll forgive me," said the voice.

I checked myself for injuries and, finding none, I straightened myself and said, "Are you Alfie?"

"Last I checked!" he said cheerfully. "Oh, and by the way, have you realized that when you fall, you land exactly like a cat?"

"I do?"

"Yes, it's quite interesting to watch. You are a very graceful person, I've gotta say," said Alfie.

"Thanks?" I said.

"Don't mention it. The pleasure is all mine," said Alfie.

I was so startled—and also sort of thrilled—that Alfie had finally shown himself that I almost forgot that I had a list—a long one—of questions that I wanted to ask. I dug that out of my pocket and looked at it for a bit. Then I looked at one of my AC/DC posters, which was the place where I thought Alfie's voice was coming from, and said, "Alfie, I have a list of inquiries here. Would you mind being subjected to intense interrogation and a lot of curiosity?"

"Nope!" said Alfie. I could practically hear the exclamation mark in his voice.

I cleared my throat and glanced at my list again. "All right. Firstly, who or what are you; why are you here; how are you communicating with Paco and me; and is the stuff in this old book I checked out at the library real?"

"Well, I'm a house spirit, as you should already know. I'm technically dead, but I'm one of those fellers who stay on Earth. You might know us as 'ghosts,'" said Alfie. "When I was alive, I was actually a guy named Emperor Marcus Aurelius, as you may be shocked to hear."

"Marcus Aurelius?" I said. "Isn't that the dude who wrote a whole book of notes on philosophy and life and stuff?"

"That's me," said Alfie. "Those notes were from when I was feeling suddenly philosophical. Most of the time, though, I was just your typical Roman guy. Of course, the gladiator fights were always a little too gory for me, but I quite enjoyed the theatre. I found the actors to be very good."

"Go on," I said, scribbling this all down in a notebook.

"So after I died, I told the folks in the Ghost Realm that I really wanted to stay and help serve humanity, blah, blah, blah —I remember giving a really inspiring speech and giving out free cookies afterward—so they made me a house spirit. They made me a house spirit during the time when Native Americans lived here, without those nasty settlers messing with their traditional way of life. I knew it seemed silly, a Roman emperor becoming the spirit of a Native American wigwam, so I decided to change my name to Alfie.

"Now, I should probably explain about house spirits. The Native Americans in this area, like many other cultures at the time, believed in spirits. Good, bad, and cotton candy-loving spirits. They had house spirits, which protected their homes from evil. But, as time passed, fewer and fewer people believed this. So for quite a long time, I was the spirit of a rabbit burrow. The baby bunnies were really very adorable, you know, but after about a hundred years of being the guardian of the same rabbit hole, watching the rabbits do all of the same things, it got kind of boring, especially for an ex-emperor who was used to a life of pizzazz and wow. But then a family of German immigrants came along—in about the year 1871, I believe. I could be wrong. Ghosts don't have a very good sense of time. Anyway . . .

usually the German immigrants settled in the Great Plains, but not all of them. This family was in the latter group. They came here and built this very house that you are in. In fact, this room is that same room that the youngest member of the family slept in. Of course, back then the house wasn't as snazzy, but renovations have been made throughout the years."

"Wait," I said. "Is this the story about the family that went missing? It's *real*?"

"Yes, of course it's real. It's as real as you are. Now let me finish."

"Sorry," I said.

"Oh, that's quite all right. Now, these immigrants were known as the Schaffer family, and they were a rather large group. Two sets of grandparents, one aunt, two uncles, the parents, several cousins who were all rather annoying, three kids, and the most adorable dog you ever did see. A French poodle, I believe. I was actually quite fond of it, and very sad when it passed away. The Schaffers, like most people, did not believe in house spirits, but their youngest daughter, Gertrud, had epilepsy and was prone to violent seizures. So I remained a house spirit to secretly watch over Gertrud and protect her. Many years passed, until one day the family all died," Alfie continued.

I looked up. "Wait a minute, *died?* The book says that they disappeared!"

"Well, your book is wrong, because they did die. It was poison in their food. The Schaffers were a very rich family, and the butler was very poor. Naturally, the butler wanted their fortune. Poisoning was a very popular method in my time. Anyway, years passed, and no one moved into the house. But one fateful day in the spring of 1960, a new family moved in. This family was known as the Weldons. They were much smaller than the Schaffers' family—only three people: the mom, the dad, and their son, Richard. And no one moved out," Alfie finished. "This is why I can communicate with you; I have a deep connection with your family."

Richard was my father's father, so Alfie had lived with four generations of my family already. He probably knew more about them than I did. Scratch that—he definitely knew more about them than I did. Dad never talked about his family. Of course, Dad never talked about much except in grunts that, despite thirteen years of life, I still couldn't interpret.

"Wow," I said. "Okay. I wasn't expecting that." I jotted *"Special Familial Connection To Alfie"* in my notebook and underlined it. "But what about Paco? Why did you reach out to him first?"

"Simple, my dear Cassidy," said Alfie. "You see, I tried to connect to you first, but you did not believe in anything supernatural or magical. You were a firm realist. But Pac-Man does believe in magic. Well, more specifically, good and bad luck. But luck is still a form of magic. Plus, his parents just died a few years ago, so he's still haunted by their deaths. Therefore, it was quite easy to make him believe. So when he visited you, your realist personality started to shift a little bit at a time, until my dear friend Sally was able to talk to you and then, eventually, me."

"Oh," I said. "I thought it was because you didn't like me." I had some questions about whether Sally was a more adept ghost-to-person communicator than Alfie, but I figured it would be rude to suggest such a thing.

"Oh, quite the contrary!" said Alfie.

"Good." I put this down in my notebook, too, and went on to the next question. "Alfie, why do you call Paco *Pac-Man*?"

"Because the first three letters of his name are 'Pac,' and, well, that just made me think Pac-Man. He didn't seem to mind the nickname, though."

"Alfie, you're Roman. How can you know about Pac-Man?"

"That's a wonderful question, Cassidy. I'm delighted you asked!" said Alfie excitedly. "I recently became aware of a little tiny thing called the Internet. Have you heard of it?"

"I have," I said. I didn't tell him that *everybody* had heard of the Internet by now.

"Excellent! Well, I found out about a website called Wikipedia, and I did some random searching. That's how I know about Pac-Man. But I also found out—and get this!—that President Kennedy is dead! *Dead!* Oh, the tragedy!"

"JFK has been dead for a long, long time now, Alfie," I said. "He was assassinated in 1963. How can you not have known of his death until now?"

"I was, uh, taking a light snooze at the time of his death. And pretty soon after he died and I woke up, people just kind of stopped talking about him, you know? So I never knew what became of him until years later. You know, presidents have always confused me, since Romans didn't really do democracy."

"That makes sense," I said. "Romans had emperors, not presidents. I can imagine how it would be slightly difficult to adjust." I wondered if Alfie would have been elected if he had been a leader in a democracy. I kind of doubted it.

"Do you have any other inquiries?" Alfie asked.

I thought for a second. "Nope. Thanks for your time."

"No problemo," said Alfie. With that, he left my mind.

After this little encounter with my long-deceased guardian, we started having little meetings every day. We called this the Ghost Club because Alfie insisted. Mostly we talked about small, trivial things such as Roman cuisine and my favorite kind of donut. Pretty soon, I became fast friends with the ghost, and I drew a picture of Alfie (with him providing the details of his physical appearance) and put it on the ceiling so I could pretend to be actually looking at him when we spoke. Sometimes, we'd play a game of chess (turned out Alfie had a few spiritual powers that allowed him to move small objects), and usually he'd win. We spent long afternoons chatting away like old friends, and just for those daily sessions with my new ghostly therapist, I'd forget about my woes and troubles, as they say, and lose myself in Alfie's babbling.

And pretty soon, it was the day before Christmas Eve.

I was talking with Alfie when a question suddenly popped into my mind. "Alfie," I said, "what happens when you die?"

"That's a very good question, Cassidy, and fortunately, one that I have an answer to," said Alfie. "You see, when you die, everything goes dark for a few minutes. But then you get a tingling sensation in your tummy, and for people with sensitive stomachs, they might experience mild nausea. Then, Beethoven's 'Für Elise' suddenly blares, and everything goes light. And you hear a sucking noise, which is your soul detaching from your body. Then you rise to the sky. If you're under a ceiling, you may hit your head a bit, but that shouldn't be much of a problem, as it's not easy for ghosts to get injured. And then, you enter the gates of the Ghost Realm, where you get registered as a dead person and assigned a place to live, either in the Ghost Realm, Heaven, or Hell."

"Question," I said. "What's the difference between the Ghost Realm and Heaven and Hell?"

"Well, Cassidy, that's another great question," said Alfie. "The Ghost Realm includes Heaven and Hell, but it's also a place itself. The Ghost Realm is the place where all of the spirits who have been both bad and good in their lives go. That includes most people. And Heaven is where all the oh-so-perfect people go. So far, that's only a couple dozen. And Hell is the place where all of the truly naughty people go. That's several hundred. Adolph Hitler and Benito Mussolini are in

Hell. You know, when Hitler first arrived in the Ghost Realm, the Jewish God Himself came down from His private palace and had a word with him. I saw it happen. God shamed Hitler right in front of everybody. It was simply delightful. By the end of it, Hitler was in tears. I had never laughed so hard in my life."

"I can imagine. Hitler was horrible," I said. "Mr. Watts goes into a rage-fueled speech whenever the guy is mentioned. Most of his family was killed in World War II."

"A true tragedy. So, Cassidy, that's what happens when a person dies," Alfie concluded. "Any more questions?"

"Yes," I said. "What happened to the ghosts of the Schaffer family?"

"Well, most of them moved on to the Ghost Realm. The French poodle went to Animal Heaven. Animal Heaven, because I can tell you're curious, is an unpolluted place untouched by humans, where the souls of departed animals go. It's basically animal paradise. But one human member of the family, for some reason, was denied entrance into the Ghost Realm. I think it's some kind of mistake. Even the extremely efficient system that all of the ghosts have to go through has flaws."

"Which member was left behind?" I asked.

"The girl with epilepsy, Gertrud. She still remains here in this house. She died at midnight on Christmas Day, so that is when she appears to haunt this house. But really, she isn't that scary. She's just a twelve-year-old ghost girl who couldn't get to where she belongs."

"Is there any way she can get back to the Ghost Realm?"

"Possibly . . . " Alfie mused. "It would have to be a human with an aura of death to escort her back. But where do I find a human with an aura of death?"

"I don't know," I said. "What does an aura of death look like?"

"Kind of a dark blue. It also smells like almonds," said Alfie.

"Like cyanide?"

"Yeah." Alfie paused. Then there was a sound like some-body snapping their fingers, and a second later, Alfie exclaimed, "I've got it! *You'll* be the one to escort Gertrud to the Ghost Realm!"

"*Me?*" I said. "But . . . why me?"

"You have an aura of death and a rather strong one, since you're due to die soon," said Alfie, "and you're one of the only people who know of the Ghost Realm and Gertrud. It makes sense for you to help Gertrud."

Now, I had known I would probably die relatively young, but still, it's one thing to know a thing and another entirely to hear it so matter-of-factly. But despite the fact that Alfie and I had become friends, good friends even, I didn't really think now was the time for me to discuss my impending death with him. Instead, I pondered the more curious thing he'd said and wondered if I smelled like almonds to everyone. "Well . . . " I said. "I don't know. Will it be dangerous?"

"Possibly," said Alfie, "but you're a very brave young lady. I'm sure you'll manage."

Brave? Alfie thought I was *brave?* That was a nice thought, but honestly, I was actually afraid of many things, including roller coasters, butterflies, small, cramped spaces, and clowns, to name a few, not to mention my extreme fear of heights. But then I thought of poor Gertrud and how horrible it must be separated from your family for eternity, and I made up my mind.

"Okay," I told Alfie. "I guess I'll do it."

"Great! But maybe you should bring Paco along," Alfie suggested.

I snorted. "*Paco?* Why?"

"Pac-Man never got to say goodbye to his parents when

they died," said Alfie. "It would be a nice thing to do for him. Besides, it's always always a good idea to have company when visiting the Ghost Realm, as it's easy to get lost there."

"Oh, fine," I said. "I suppose he can come along."

"That's the spirit! Now, here's what you have to do . . . "

CHAPTER

FIVE

Z E DAY KNOWN AS CHRISTMAS EVE
I called Paco to let him know that I was traveling to the land of the dead and ask if he would like to come along. I also told him I didn't think he was mentally ill anymore. He accepted and proceeded to ramble on and on and on and on about the decreasing quality of the Happy Meals at McDonald's for about eleven minutes before I ended the call.

It was going to be a long trip.

Then I began to prepare for the arrival of Gertrud.

First, I hunted for bright clothing in my room so that I could draw the ghosts' attention. That feat wasn't too hard because my Aunt Lucy was under the illusion that I liked wearing neon and glittery stuff a lot (actually, I preferred more neutral colors). Then I got out several candles that I planned to arrange in a circle, and I put a nightlight beside my bed. I looked at the picture of Alfie pasted on my ceiling and I mentally thanked him for his assistance. Then I went downstairs to check that there were still a bunch of Sprites in the fridge.

There were none.

I groaned. I would have to go to Walmart to get some more, and I really didn't want to go outside right now, as it was a total blizzard and probably pretty darn cold. But I needed Sprite to summon Gertrud, so I reluctantly dressed in several heavy coats, three pairs of socks, the tallest, most insulated boots I could find, and a warm knitted hat. I borrowed Mr. Watt's credit card and stepped outside.

Immediately, I knew that I'd made the right decision to dress like the world was coming to an end in a great big avalanche. The wind howled and stung, biting my skin and blowing my hair back. The ground was covered in about ten inches of snow. I pulled my hat down over my ears and started walking to Walmart.

By the time I arrived at my destination, I was a soaked, miserable green-haired mess.

Safely inside the store, I pulled off my hat, which made my hair stand up with static, and shook the snow off of my clothes. Then I went searching for a twelve-pack of Sprite because I was actually craving the sugary, sweet drink today.

I found the Sprite next to a bunch of other sodas. Unlucky for me, though, it was on a shelf a little too high for me to reach.

As I contemplated this unfortunate occurrence, the person next to me, who had been looking at the different kinds of Coke, reached over my head and pulled the Sprite off the shelf, "Here ya go," they said, setting it in my cart.

"Thank you so much!" I said. But then I recognized the person. No, it was not Paco. It was somebody much better. "X!"

"Hey, Cassidy," said X, winking. They pointed at the Sprite and said, "I see that you're attempting to summon a ghost, huh?"

I nodded. "Yeah, I am."

"Cool! Tell me if it works, a'ight? I wanna know if ghosts really do love Sprite," X said.

I laughed. "Okay, I will!" I thought about inviting X along on our trip, but I was already going to have to explain Paco's presence to my parents, and I didn't really know if there was a visitor limit on my aura of death thing or whatever.

I said goodbye to X and bought the Sprite, then lugged it all the way back home with me. The freezing weather kept the soda cold, but it nearly froze my hands off. I breathed a sigh of relief, glad to be back home. I put the Sprite in the refrigerator, then pulled all of my warm garments off. I collapsed on the couch. "Oh, man, that's so much better," I groaned.

Ding-skkkkrreeeeeccccccchhh! went the doorbell. I jumped up immediately and raced to answer it.

"Hello, Paco," I said, opening the door.

"Hey, Cassidy," said Paco, shivering. "Man, it's *cold* out!"

"Yes, I know; I just came back from the grocery store a few minutes ago," I said. "Come in and shut the door behind you."

"Okay," said Paco. He quickly closed the door, then took off his coat, hat, and boots. "I think I'm in the mood for a hot chocolate."

"Well, you're in luck," I told him. "The cook, Frances, is frothing the milk as we speak. She makes the best hot chocolate because she puts in whipped cream, cinnamon, a dash of allspice, a stick of peppermint candy, and really, really, really frothy milk. Delicious."

"Can't wait to try it," said Paco. "Hey, are your parents around? I wanna meet them."

"No, you do not," I said. "The person you want to meet is Mr. Watts, my Polish comedian caretaker and one of the best people on Earth."

"Why can't I meet your parents?" Paco asked.

"Because they are not nice people. They abandoned me, for goodness' sake. They are terrible parents!"

"Well, how was I supposed to know that?" said Paco. "You never told me anything about your parents."

He had a point, but I was grumpy with nerves and the lack of parental holiday spirit, so I just mumbled something like, "Because that is a very sore subject for me. Now, come and meet Mr. Watts."

After receiving our hot chocolates, Paco and I went around to meet everyone. Paco loved Mr. Watts, had a whole conversation in Spanish with Chelsea, showed Frances how to make churros and enchiladas, and even danced to Mediterranean music with our Cuban maid. I was a little jealous of him because he got along so well with everyone after only a few minutes of knowing them.

Then we went up to my room.

"Hi, Pac-Man," said Alfie when we came to my room. "Lovely to see you again."

"Hi, Alfie!" Paco said. He air-hugged Alfie—an air-hug because it's not easy hugging a person who's been dead for centuries and appears only as a voice, without any sort of body. Paco grinned. "So I understand we're trying to summon a ghost named Gertrud who has been prevented from entering the Ghost Realm and attempt to take her to where she belongs?"

"That's exactly right!" Alfie said. "You are not exactly required in the process—"

This made Paco's happy expression deteriorate.

"But I think you would probably like to see your parents again," said Alfie.

This made Paco's frown transform into a giddy smile. "I can see my parents again?!" he squealed. Yes, he actually did squeal. It was very funny to witness, and it also brought a tear to my left eye.

"Yeah, you can," I said.

"Oh my goodness gracious, I can't believe how lucky I am!" Paco said without taking a breath. He sank to his knees and said, "Alfie, thank you so, so, so, so, so, so, so, so much! I am forever in your debt!" Then he got back up and jumped up and down in excitement, yelling things in Norwegian. Then he calmed down, sat on the edge of my bed, and said, "So I suppose I'll be staying the night."

"Yup," I said.

"I just need to call my abuelita to make sure it's okay with her," said Paco. He took out his phone, which had a smiley face sticker slapped onto the back, punched in a phone number, and proceeded to have a rapid conversation with his grandmother in Spanish.

I waited patiently for the call to end, sipping my hot chocolate and staring at the ceiling. Finally, Paco slid his cell phone into his jeans pocket and said, "She says it's fine for me to stay over. She's with my cousins for Christmas, and she says as long as I'm there for dinner tomorrow at noon, I'm good."

"Alrighty!" Alfie said. "Pac-Man, do you know what happens when you die? It's not something you easily forget . . . "

I finished my hot chocolate and took the empty mug downstairs while Alfie filled my very tall Mexican-Norwegian sort-of friend in on what to expect in the afterlife. I rinsed it out and put it in the dishwasher. Frances was perfecting her enchiladas, a recipe she now knew, thanks to Paco.

"Hey, Frances," I said as I watched her cook. "Is that for lunch?"

Frances chuckled and shook her head. "Naw, just a little

somethin' I'm cookin' up for fun. That boy you brought over sure knows how to make a good enchilada."

"Paco," I reminded her. "His name is Paco."

"Right, sorry. I'm not very good with names," she said. "Where'd you meet him, anyhow?"

I decided not to tell her that he just came into my house without permission when I was all alone, so I just lied and said, "We met at the library. He works there."

Frances eyed me. She could always tell whenever I was lying, but she never tried to press for answers. "The library, huh."

"Yeah," I said. "The library."

"Okay, whatever you say," she said and turned back to her enchiladas.

I went back upstairs, where Paco and Alfie were still chatting away like old friends. I had to take my medicine, so I veered toward the bathroom.

"Cassidy!" Alfie called.

I stopped. "What?"

"Where are you going?"

"To the bathroom," I said, "duh."

"Why?"

"To take my medicine," I told him.

"Don't do that!" said Alfie, sounding panicked.

"Why not?" I asked.

"If you take your medicine, it'll prevent you from journeying to the Ghost Realm," said Alfie. "Although it does slow your eventual death, it also keeps you in the mortal realm. You have to fall into a self-induced coma to enter if you're alive—"

"I have to *what?*" I interrupted. "I'm sorry, but I don't think you ever mentioned that before!"

"—and that medicine of yours will stop that," Alfie barged

on, ignoring me, "so please don't take it. All will be lost if you do!"

"That sounds like something a character from *Geronimo Stilton: The Kingdom of Fantasy* would say. The Kingdom of Fantasy series was all about saving people from certain death," I said, but I turned back and went into my room.

People wake up from comas all the time, I reminded myself, a little unconvincingly.

The rest of the day passed without incident. Paco and I each consumed three Sprites (we still had six left; don't worry) and played chess. I beat him most of the time because he was absolutely hopeless at the game. We also watched *Hocus Pocus 2*, which had just come out, and which I was excited to watch. Alfie remained silent most of the time, except to keep score of how many times Paco lost to me at chess (it was nine times). Finally, night fell and everyone else went to bed.

I watched the clock on my dresser tick closer and closer to midnight to take advantage of the thinnest time of the veil for my first trip across. I had arranged my candles in a circle, which Paco and I sat inside. I wore my most neon clothes: a glow-in-the-dark green raincoat, pink glittery high-tops, which I absolutely loathed because of their offensive color, and a pair of shimmery purple leggings. Paco wore his usual white shirt with the words "Bob's Hardware and Appliances" printed on the back and a pair of blue jeans.

The clock hit 11:55.

11:56.

11:57.

11:58.

11:59.

I squeezed Paco's hand tightly, which somehow my hand had found of its own accord. He squeezed it back even harder, making my knuckles crack. I extracted my hand so as to prevent further injuries and glared at the clock even harder. I had been working on my eye-popping techniques, and as of this moment, they were probably bulging out of my sockets.

12:00.

Instead of relaxing, I tensed up even further. It was midnight; now we just had to see if the ghost would come.

My long, pointy nose suddenly caught a whiff of almonds, and I could see a little puff of dark blue through the crack I had left in my door. I mouthed to Paco, "She's here," but honestly, that was kind of unnecessary as he'd already seen the blue haze.

The candles surrounding us blew out, leaving us in the dark, except for my rain jacket.

A large ball of white light floated through the door, the blue aura of death following it. The light stopped right in front of us, illuminating its surroundings. I caught a glimpse of Paco's face, bathed in the white light. He looked terrified.

Slowly, the light started to take shape until it morphed into two figures: a girl and an old man.

The old man looked a lot like the drawing on my ceiling. He had a gray, curly beard, some serious sideburns, short silvery hair, a kindly smile on his wrinkled face, and a toga. The girl was shorter than him and seemed to be about my age. She had pale blond hair plaited into long braids that hung past her shoulders, gray eyes, a lacy, frilly nightdress, and very pale skin. Both had a grayish pallor to their skin and were slightly transparent.

"Hello, Cassidy," the old man spoke. "I'm Alfie, if you haven't recognized me already, and this is Gertrud."

We stammered out a hello, and Gertrud just looked at us with no change to her expression.

"Gertrud," said Alfie, "don't be rude; say hello to Cassidy and Paco here."

"Hello, Cassidy and Paco," Gertrud said to us. Her voice was high and wispy, with a trace of a German accent. "Have you really come to help me? Will I get to see my family again?"

I swallowed my fear and said in my most comforting voice (which, admittedly, wasn't all that comforting), "Yes, Gertrud. To both of those questions. We're here to take you home." I elbowed Paco in the side swiftly but inconspicuously to un-petrify him.

He looked like a very, very tall statue.

"Get ahold of yourself," I hissed at him and turned back to the ghosts. "So, Alfie, how do we fall into self-induced comas?"

"Oh, it's fairly easy," said Alfie, "First, you lie down on your back. Then you think of a bunch of pleasant things, like peach cobbler, ice cream with sprinkles, the smell of the ocean, being on the good side of the Senate, horses, alpacas, or the hope that the apocalypse will not occur for at least another thousand years. Then you clear your mind of everything, close your eyes, and stare into the black nothingness behind your eyelids. And you just remain that way for a little while . . ." [1]

Alfie's voice faded away, and I felt very peaceful. I guess I fell into that coma because the next thing I saw when I opened my eyes was a dude behind a desk with a name tag that read in fancy cursive letters *Greg*♥. Paco and Gertrud stood right next to me, and behind us, a long line of ghosts stretched, waiting patiently for their turn.

I quickly took in the place where I was. We were standing in a gigantic, cavernous room that could've been a lobby of a massive office complex if it weren't so huge. There were multiple benches where some people sat, and there were hundreds of gigantic glass chandeliers adorning the ceiling. The whole "lobby" was different shades of gray, and the only things that were colorful were Paco and me.

The guy behind the desk, Greg, stared at my colorful clothing. "Guest, eh?" he said, typing something into the computer in front of him. He wore a fancy tweed business suit, and his shiny grayish-blond hair was slicked back. He looked like a guy from the mid-1900s.

"Guest?" I said, confused.

Greg sighed. "*Guest* is the ghost slang term for folks who've fallen into comas. When humans fall into comas, they are temporarily transported to the Ghost Realm. Of course, some people never wake up from their comas, so they are permanently transported to the Ghost Realm. That's how I died."

"Oh," I said. "Well, in that case, yes, I am a guest. So is my friend here." I motioned toward Paco. "Gertrud is a ghost, though," I added, pointing at her.

Greg squinted at her. "She don't look like a new ghost."

"Nope," I agreed. "She died in 18—uh, let's see, 1874. Yup."

"Ah, she's one of those who've slipped past our system?" Greg asked.

"Yeah," I said. "Seriously, man, you need to improve your system here. There are probably hundreds of ghosts worldwide who haven't gotten to the Ghost Realm."

"I know," Greg sighed again. "It's quite unfortunate. I believe some of our ghosts are working on the solution. Thank you for bringing Gertrud back."

"You're welcome. Do you know where in the Ghost Realm her family is?"

"Well, what's her last name?"

"Schaffer."

"Oh, we've got tons and tons of those," said Greg, tapping on the computer keyboard. He looked at Gertrud and asked, "What're your parents' names, sweetie?"

"Greta Schultz Schaffer and Fritz Schaffer," Gertrud answered.

"Now we've narrowed it down to a couple of them. What do they look like?"

"They look like me, except that my father has brown hair and my mother has brown eyes," said Gertrud.

"Ah, yes, now I know which Schaffers you're talking about," said Greg. He pounded a few more keys and announced, "They reside in apartment six, Leafy Elm Hollow Apartment Complex, 1039th St, in the Ghost Realm. Here's a map." He handed me a huge map, and I blinked. The Ghost Realm was, to put it simply, enormous. I mean, I knew that it was going to be big—where would all of those souls go?—but this was way bigger than I had been expecting.

"In each of your pockets," Greg went on, "you have a thousand dollars' worth of joss paper, which is the currency of the Ghost Realm. Not the whole Ghost Realm, mind you; Heaven has golden coins with trees engraved on them because Heaven is all about trees, and Hell uses accordion keys. You also have free access to all of the hot dogs you want."

"What are hot dogs?" Gertrud asked.

"Something wonderful and yummy, trust me," I said.

"That's exactly right," said Greg.

We bumped fists—I was starting to like this guy—and then Greg said, "Well, y'all have a good time in the Ghost Realm, all right? Gimme a call if you need anything—my phone number is there on that map—and don't forget to try the hot dogs!"

"We won't," I told him. He grinned and pointed toward a door to the left and informed us that it led to the rest of the Ghost Realm. Then he wished us luck and moved on to the next person in line, a woman with a lilac-purple mohawk and a nose piercing.

We went through the door and found ourselves standing on a wide street. I looked behind me and saw that we'd walked through what looked like a mansion. Trees were everywhere, flowering even though it was winter and snow was falling. A few cars went past.

I could see how this place was for the people who'd been neither good nor bad in their lifetimes. It was a pleasant place, but not perfect either. I noticed that there were no animals because all of the animals were in their own little afterlife. There was no birdsong, which was slightly depressing because I like birdsong. Beyond the quaint little houses, there were taller buildings—apartment complexes, probably.

I'd given the map to Paco, and now he was examining it, muttering to himself.

"Hey," I said. "Have you found where Leafy Elm Hollow is?"

"Yeah," he said. He pointed to a place on the map. "It's actually not too far."

I turned to Gertrud. "Gertrud, are you excited that you're going to see your family again?"

The ghost girl was bouncing up and down on the balls of her feet. "Yes, yes, yes! I am so happy! Thank you, thank you, thank you! When do we get there?"

"Soon," I said.

Gertrud hugged me, a hug that was surprisingly solid, though it did feel slightly chilly, but that was because she was a ghost. I hugged her back, and then we started on our quest to find Leafy Elm Hollow Apartment Complex.

We walked past ghosts from many different time frames— once, I thought I saw Benjamin Franklin signing the autograph of a red-haired kid wearing a backwards baseball hat. Around another corner, I bumped into a man wearing a red tunic over a suit of chainmail with pointy boots and leggings. We followed Paco, turning down different streets and alleys. Eventually, Leafy Elm Hollow came into view. It was actually more like a large Victorian mansion than an apartment building, but there was a parking lot in front. Leafy Elm Hollow was, in fact, not surrounded by elms—it was surrounded by red oaks. I found that a little disconcerting.

Greeting us at the entrance of Leafy Elm Hollow was a woman with big square glasses, a pageboy cut, and a blue V-neck sweater. She looked us over with a frown that seemed to be her primary expression and said in a British accent, "Whaddya want?"

"We're here to see the Schaffer family," I explained.

"We have three Schaffer families in this complex," said the woman. "You'll have to elaborate."

"Uh, the really big Schaffer family in apartment six," I said.

"Oh, *that* one," she said. "Follow me, then."

The woman led us up several flights of stairs, and then we made two right turns and walked down the hall until we came to apartment six. The woman motioned at the door, said, "Go on in," and disappeared elsewhere.

I let Gertrud open the door since this was her family. She grabbed ahold of the bronze doorknob, wrenched the door open with so much force that I was afraid that it had been ripped off of its hinges, and ran inside, screaming her parents' names. "*Mother! Father!*"

Everyone inside apartment six turned their heads in her direction. "*GERTRUD?!*" they all said in unison.

There was silence for a few moments.

Then all of the Schaffers ran and swept Gertrud up in a gigantic group hug.

"Where have you *been?!*" one of her cousins demanded.

The aunt and all of the uncles were bawling into their handkerchiefs loudly, overjoyed that their darling Gertrud was back. One of the two sets of grandparents was squeezing her so tightly that her eyes were bulging even further than mine had when she'd first appeared.

Finally, a couple that was not exactly elderly but not exactly young either battled their way through the crowd of Schaffers. I guessed they were Gertrud's mother and father, because they looked more like her than the others, and because they were so desperate to get to her.

"Mother! Father!" Gertrud yelled again.

Gertrud's parents cried out, "**Gertrud!**" and began fussing over her, asking how things had been going for her for the past 148 years. Paco and I stood awkwardly in the doorway, watching this show of parental love. I was happy for Gertrud, really, I was, but my heart ached a little. It had been so long since my own parents had shown me this kind of love. I realized I missed having decent parents much more than I thought I did. A lump formed in my throat, and I fought back tears.

Gertrud managed to extract herself from her parents' arms and pointed at us. "Mother, Father, these people helped me find you. Without them, I might still be trapped on Earth."

"Well, technically we're still on Earth. The Ghost Realm is in the troposphere, which is part of Earth's atmosphere," Gertrud's dad began, but her mom shushed him.

Everyone in the room turned to look at us, and I felt myself blush a deep shade of crimson.

"Did you really bring our Gertrud back to us?" Gertrud's mother asked.

I nodded.

All of the Schaffers, even the grandparents who hobbled around on canes, surged forward like paparazzi rushing to bother a celebrity. There was lots of cheering, and I found myself being tossed in the air by a couple of burly teenage boys, which wasn't so great since I was afraid of heights. Oh, boy.

Gertrud finally got everyone calmed down enough to sit down and listen to what she had to say. She looked at Paco and me with a grateful smile, and said, "My friends, thank you so much for reuniting me with my family. I am forever in your debt."

This made me blush even more, and made Paco smile shyly. "It was our pleasure," I stammered out. "Um . . . we gotta go, but we're really happy that you're happy."

The Schaffers cheered and bade us farewell. Before we went, we heard Gertrud's mother gushing about the quality of the hot dogs. The door slammed shut, and suddenly silence reigned in the hall.

I looked at Paco, and he looked at me. "Well," I said, "what're we waiting for? Let's go find your parents."

CHAPTER
SIX

We figured out where Paco's parents were—Nightingale Cove—but that was too far to walk, so instead, we got on a bus that was heading for Nightingale Cove. We sat next to an old lady knitting a sweater with something called Cloud Yarn (apparently, it was yarn made from clouds, as I learned when I asked her what it was). Across from us was a gay couple snuggling with each other, and next to the couple was a person with cornrows tapping away on their phone. The bus rumbled along a gravelly road, causing Paco and me to bounce up and down in our seats.

Nightingale Cove was not an actual cove, as we found out from the gay couple, who just happened to live there. It was a cozy cluster of cottages surrounded by huge chestnut trees, like a Robin Hood village, and the only reason it was called Nightingale Cove was because it was a nice name.

The bus turned, and suddenly we were covered by the shadows of the massive trees that towered above us. It wasn't snowing in this part of the Ghost Realm; in fact, it was actually pretty warm. It felt more like summer than winter.

"Nearly there," the bus driver announced.

I felt Paco tense up with excitement beside me. I instinctively put my hand on his arm, and he flinched a bit.

"Sorry," I said, removing it.

"S'okay," he said quietly, turning to look out of the window.

"Paco, are you okay? You've been awfully quiet ever since we arrived in the Ghost Realm," I said.

"I'm fine. I've just been . . . thinking," Paco said.

"About your parents?" I guessed.

He nodded. "Yeah. It's been three years, and I've grown a lot. I don't know if they'll recognize me or not."

"Oh," I said. "I get it now." I had wondered the same thing when my parents had been gone a long time, but of course, my parents hadn't died. It wasn't the same, but for a minute, my situation felt pretty terrible. I didn't say that.

We didn't talk for the rest of the bus ride. Instead, we absorbed the beauty of the forest around us. It was almost like the forest at home. I kept expecting deer to jump out at any minute, but animals didn't exist here.

"Here we are, folks," the bus driver called. "Nightingale Cove is just to the left."

The bus stopped, and we clambered out and headed left toward what looked like a big log cabin in the woods. It was surrounded by trees, and there was a little stream running out front. There were a few other cabins, all slightly different, scattered around. The only thing missing from this sort of perfect forest-y place were chipmunks. To be perfect, it definitely needed chipmunks—or at least a squirrel or something.

As we walked up the path to the cabin, I wondered who had decided animals got their own heaven. Of course, the situation was great for the animals because I was fairly certain that most of their suffering on Earth was caused by humans, but I couldn't help but feel the realm of ghosts was a little less than ideal without animals. In fact, it felt downright bleak to not see them.

And I knew the bleakness of life without animals since my parents had never let me have even a guinea pig. Once, Mr. Watts had brought home a kitten for me, but I slipped up in one of my letters to my parents and mentioned Mycroft the Cat (his full name), and the next day, Frances had taken the cat home with her for her daughter. "I'm sorry, Miss Cassidy," Frances had said, "I can't lose my job."

Thinking about Mycroft the Cat made me sad, but it was better than thinking about absent parents. But it was even better to think about the lumberjacks who had cut down the logs for this massive house. They must have been huge, like Paul Bunyan. I wondered if Paul Bunyan lived in the realm of ghosts. I knew he was a legend, but most legends had their roots in history, so it was possible.

By the time we reached the porch of the immense log cabin, I was on high alert for signs of a huge lumberjack or a gigantic blue ox, and I was so absorbed in my search that I almost missed the quirky fact that the doorbell of the house was shaped like a saxophone.

Paco was smiling and crying at the same time as he pushed the illuminated saxophone, and when a woman with long dark hair and dark skin and a man with a blond puff of hair like Paco's opened the door, he almost jumped through the door. "Mama, Papa!" he shouted.

Because Paco was taller than both his parents and had caught them off guard, he knocked them both down with his exuberance, and I started laughing so hard that I had to lean against the door frame to keep from falling over. I thought it was probably rude to be lying down when I met my best friend's parents.

I couldn't begin to explain how Paco had become my best friend, but as soon as I thought about it, I knew I was right. Of course, I was right most of the time, say about ninety-two percent of the time, so that wasn't really surprising.

Once the Solbergs got to their feet and hugged a bit more but less awkwardly, I cleared my throat in the universal signal of "Hey, remember, I'm back here."

"Oh, Mom and Dad, this is my friend Cassidy." He stepped to the side and waved his arm like he was a magician and I, his assistant. I made a mental note to talk about the hierarchy of our friendship at a more appropriate time.

"Hi, Mr. and Mrs. Solberg—is that what I should call you?" I asked.

"That's perfect, Cassidy. It's nice to meet you. Would you like to come in?" Mrs. Solberg said. She had a faint accent that told of her native country.

Paco, having tackled his parents only a few moments ago, was already inside, and I didn't see any reason I shouldn't follow suit. I walked into the gorgeous log cabin and smiled. "Did you design your own home?" I said.

Mr. Solberg nodded. "It's a perk of the realm. Custom designs for everyone."

I pondered that as Mr. Solberg took us on a tour. Had Gertrud's family wanted an apartment? I wondered. I'm not sure I'd pick an apartment, but log cabins weren't really my speed either. I made another mental note to think more carefully about my Ghost Realm living experience so I would be ready when the time came. Maybe a loft in a converted factory? I had a lot of thinking to do.

The tour took about thirty minutes and involved far more detail about the insulation and window glass than I had been expecting, but Paco seemed happy to just be with his parents. I found that his happiness made me happy too.

We sat in the family room, which gave me a hunter-ish vibe because of the stuffed moose head above the fireplace (poor moose) and the pine walls (it smelled really great, too). We sipped iced tea and ate some cookies Mr. Solberg had made, and Paco told his parents all about the book and Alfie and my house. He even told them I was his best friend, too, and that felt good, although I tried to look casual when he said it.

After a couple of hours, though, Mrs. Solberg said we needed to go. "You can't stay in a coma too long, kids." She stood and led us to the door. "It's not good for your growing brains."

I knew she had a point because my brain was starting to feel all tingly like my hand did when I slept with it all twisted up under my pillow. "Thank you for having me," I said, practicing the manners Mr. Watts had always insisted I learn. Now I knew why.

"Thank you for bringing our Paco," Mr. Solberg said as he hugged me close. "We will see you all when it's your time to build here."

I smiled and went outside to wait on the porch. I was feeling sad, and if I felt that way, I couldn't imagine how Paco must have been feeling.

A few minutes later, when he came out, his eyes were wet, but I didn't say anything. Instead, I just slung my arm over his head and said, "Last one to the bus stop has to eat a worm." I hadn't used such silly dares since first grade, but it seemed silliness was in order.

Paco seemed to appreciate the distraction because he was out ahead of me before I even got started. Darn his very long legs. He won handily, and as if on cue, the bus came up the road and stopped in front of us.

The driver was the same man as before, and I wondered if he just worked long shifts or if, maybe, he lived on the bus as his dream of being a bus driver. I almost asked him but figured that was a bit out of line, given that I didn't know the man. Another question to tuck away for my next visit, when I was good and dead. At least I had something to look forward to after death—a new house and the answers to lots and lots of questions.

Now, though, we had to do the tricky work of pulling ourselves out of a coma.

I realized that Alfie had forgotten to tell us how to wake up, and I cursed inwardly. Oh, great. I nudged Paco beside me and relayed the very bad news. He looked worried. "I've actually been aware of that for a while now, but I didn't want to worry you, because good things never happen when you're worried."

"Dang, you know me well," I said. "Well, how do you suppose we'll get home?"

Paco stroked his chin. Recently, he had started growing a goatee, as puberty had hit, so he stroked that as well. "Maybe find someone who knows what to do?"

"Okay," I said.

Once the bus driver dropped a few passengers off at some place called Ever-Winter Village (where it always seemed to be snowing), I approached him and asked, "Mister, me and my friend here are in comas; we need to wake up, and, well, we don't know how to do that. Do you know of someone who can help us?"

"As a matter o' fact, I do," he said, turning around in his seat. He had a thick Scottish accent with day-old stubble, thinning brown hair, blue eyes, and a round belly. A knit cap was pulled over his square head, and he wore Wellington boots (a necessary accessory for a Scot). "I'm William McCorkle—you can call me Will; everyone does—and I possess the knowledge ye're lookin' for. My shift ends at 12:30. Meet me at O'Riley's Pizzeria at 12:40."

"All right," I said and went back to Paco to tell him the news.

"Really?" Paco asked. "Just like that? I dunno, Cassidy. This seems kinda suspicious to me."

I shrugged. "He seems nice enough. Besides, it's not like we have any other options."

"Oh, fine," Paco sighed. "I'm getting hungry anyway."

We arrived at O'Riley's Pizzeria at exactly 12:40. The restaurant looked boring on the outside—it was basically just a box-shaped building made out of brick with the occasional graffiti—but on the inside, it was a whole 'nother world. The interior was painted a deep olive green, with plants like English ivy climbing the walls and the wood rafters that made up the ceiling. Some of the plants were flowering, filling the air with their sweet scent. There was a sign on the wall that read:

Customers Beware: Large Clouds of Pollen Released at Random Times
If you are allergic to pollen or are bothered by it in any way, you can eat outside on the patio.
Thank you!
Love, the Staff of O'Riley's Pizzeria

Buddha statues were placed around the room, with little metal elephants holding candles on every table. There was a doorway that led to the patio (I knew it led to the patio because it had a sign on it that said so), a hallway that led to what I assumed were the bathrooms, and another door that led to the kitchen. There was a wooden desk in the corner of the dining room, where a person with a bright-blue faux-hawk stood. There was also a vending machine near the bathrooms.

I spotted Will at one of the tables, and we went over to him.

His cap was off, but otherwise, he looked just the same. He had a can of Coke and was drinking deeply from it.

"Hey, Will," I said, sliding into one of the other seats at the table.

Paco sat down in the chair next to me.

Will looked up from his Coke. "Hey . . . I just realized I never got yer names."

"Cassidy," I said.

"Paco," said Paco.

"Well, in that case, hello, Miss Cassidy and Mister Paco," Will said. A waitress sauntered over with some menus, and she handed one to me and one to Paco.

After ordering our pizzas (I got barbecue because I can't resist it), we began discussing how to rouse ourselves from our comas.

"I know how to wake you up," said Will, "but I'm warning ye, it ain't cheap, and there's no guarantee that it'll work."

"There's no harm in trying," said Paco, and grabbed his wad of joss paper out of his pocket. I remembered that I'd been given some joss paper too, and I pulled that out as well. "How much do you want?"

"At least half o' what you got there," Will said, "for the both of ye."

That seemed pricey, but given that we had no choice, I passed over my half, and Paco gave his half to Will too. "There," I said. "Now what do we have to do?"

"Well, how'd ye fall into those comas anyhow?" Will asked.

"We thought of pleasant things, then cleared our minds and just . . . fell asleep," I answered.

"You do sup'm similar in wakin' up," said Will, "'cept you don't clear yer minds. Ye think of nice things, and then it just sorta . . . happens. And it doesn't always work for everybody, mind."

"Okay," I said and followed his instructions.

Nothing happened.

Disappointed, I tried again. Still nothing.

"Will," I said, "it's not working."

"That's normal," Will said. "Sorry, lass. Looks like it doesn't want to work for you."

I felt a lump in my throat again, and I swallowed hard in the feeble hope that it would disappear.

Nope.

I looked at Paco. He had his eyes shut, and I could tell that he was thinking hard. I could almost hear the gears in his brain whirring.

Then Paco opened his eyes. "Cassidy," he said, "I feel weird."

"Weird?" I asked. "How?"

"Like sort of tingly. You know, that feeling you get when your foot falls asleep?" Paco said. "I feel like that."

"Have you tried moving around a bunch?" I said.

"Yeah. It's not going away, though. I think it's getting worse," he said.

I looked closer at Paco and gasped. I wasn't one for gasping, but what was happening with Paco deserved a good, sharp intake of air. He was going all shimmery, almost transparent. I grabbed his arm. It was barely solid. When I'd last touched him, he'd felt normal. But now, it felt like my hand could pass through him.

"Paco," I said, "you're disappearing!"

"I am?"

"Yeah, just look at yourself! You're completely transparent now!"

Paco glanced at his arm. "Holy cow, you're not kidding!"

He tried to say more, but his voice was getting very faint, and I couldn't read lips, so I had no idea what he was saying.

And suddenly, with the sort of popping noise you get when you touch a balloon to a needle, he vanished into thin air.

The waitress came back with platters of pizza. Setting them down on the table, she noticed the empty chair beside me and asked, "Hey, where'd your friend go?"

"Home," I said.

She nodded and asked nothing more about him. "Do you guys need anything else?" she inquired.

I shook my head. "Nah, I think we're good, thank you."

The waitress smiled and walked away to check on two women at the next table.

Will and I ate our pizzas (ghost food was quite good), and then, once again, I attempted to wake up from my coma, to no avail. Will seemed rather nonchalant about the whole situation, and when he had to leave, I didn't object, even though I was left with the task of paying for our meal.

Then I wandered the streets, found a hot dog vendor, sat down on a nearby bench, and chowed down. I wasn't hungry, not after the big meal I'd just eaten, but I didn't think it would be easy to gain weight by eating ghost food, and there is such a thing as comfort food, you know.

While I was eating, someone with dark skin, dreadlocks, and a bright-orange backpack plopped down next to me.

I looked up from my hot dog, the tip of my nose covered in ketchup, and immediately recognized the person sitting next to me. "*X?*"

"Yup, it's me," said my non-binary fellow bibliophile friend, smiling.

"You're dead, aren't you?" I asked, suddenly feeling very sad.

X nodded, their dreadlocks flying with their head movement. "Yeah. Got run over by a truck. I was stupid, reading while walking."

I fell silent and stared at the remains of the hot dog in my hand. And then I did something I hadn't done in years; I started to cry.

Warm, salty tears ran down my cheeks, smudging my eyeshadow even more. I didn't bother to wipe it up, because it would stain my clothes, and besides, I felt like crying a river. I leaned against X and cried and cried and cried, gulping down breaths of fresh air between loud, gasping sobs. X put their arm around me, their bare skin warm against my cold body. I hadn't realized how cold I'd been until now—shivering, I hugged them tighter.

It was weird, hugging someone I barely even knew, but as of that moment, I didn't even care. I was lost in my sorrow. As I wept, I wished my parents would act like parents should. I wished I were going to real school and making real friends. I wished so many things, things that I didn't even know I'd wanted. But most of all, I wished I didn't have this stupid disease that was preventing me from doing so many things.

Slowly my tears started to dry up. By then, a puddle had formed at my feet, soaking into the dirt beneath my shoes.

Now all I was doing was hyperventilating, gasping, and making weird noises. X pulled away and wiped at my tears with the hem of their shirt. I managed to choke out a thank you, and they said, "Of course, sweetheart, of course."

My breathing gradually became more normal, and the lump in my throat went away. I was really, really thirsty, though.

I held X's hand, and together we sat on that bench, watching the sun descend behind the horizon. As the first stars appeared, I looked at them, and they looked at me, and we smiled.

Because right then, I felt like all was well. I felt, for the first time in many, many years, at peace.

CHAPTER
SEVEN

Eventually, X had to go; where, I couldn't say, but we both just suddenly realized they did. So with a parting hug, they left me on the bench, gazing at the stars. I sat there for a while, just looking.

I was pretty much already completely numb from my little breakdown earlier, so I didn't feel the tingling sensation throughout my body. I didn't notice as my skin turned see-through. But when I blinked, all went black.

"Hello, Cassidy," Alfie's voice boomed in my mind.

I muttered, "Hi, Alfie."

"It appears that you have succeeded in waking up from your coma," said Alfie. "I congratulate you. Also, let it be known that I take full responsibility for neglecting to give you instructions on how to wake up. I am most terribly sorry, and I promise that—"

"Alfie," I interrupted. "It's fine. You're not in trouble."

"Oh, good," he said, sounding relieved.

I smiled. "It's good to hear your voice again, Alfie. I was beginning to miss you in the Ghost Realm."

"I missed you, too!" Alfie said. "Oh, looks like they're loading you into the ambulance right now. I gotta go. For some reason, the connection right now is terrible. Gotta go! Bye, Cassidy!"

"Bye, Alfie," I said. "Wait—*ambulance?!*"

I blinked and discovered that I was no longer in the Ghost Realm. I was on a stretcher outside my house, and two men were loading me into an ambulance. My parents were nowhere around, but Mr. Watts was right next to me, looking very worried. Paco was being loaded into another ambulance a bit farther up the driveway.

"Mr. Watts?" I asked groggily.

"Cassidy!" said Mr. Watts, relieved. "Oh, am I glad to see you're awake. You were babbling nonsense about some ghost realm and being glad to see some chump named Alfie. The doctors say that your illness has finally caught up to you. I hope they're wrong; I really hope they are!"

Now that he mentioned my illness, I did feel strange, and I didn't think it was from the coma. I felt sort of happy, even though I didn't know *why* I was happy. "Mr. Watts," I said, "where's my mom?"

"In the hospital," he responded. "She's giving birth to the baby."

"Boy or girl?" I asked.

"We don't know yet. It's intersex."

"Oh," I said. I felt like singing a song, so I did. "Mary had a little lamb, little lamb, little lamb," I sang, and then I giggled hilariously. I didn't know why I did it. It occurred to me that I was finally "spiraling into insanity" like the doctors had predicted when I was eight, and this seemed very, very funny in my mind, so I giggled again. I smelled lavender and also a whiff of almond, which I knew was my death aura, and this seemed hilarious too.

Some part of me was aware that I was probably losing my grip on reality, but I didn't care, even though Mr. Watts looked terribly concerned. I just let myself laugh maniacally all the way into the ambulance and on down the road toward the hospital.

Eventually, I drifted off to sleep with a giggle on my lips. I felt insane because I just wasn't one to giggle, so when I felt myself dozing off, I didn't fight it even though I was really curious to see what was happening.

The next thing I knew, I woke up in a hospital bed with my dad sitting in a chair by my head and Mr. Watts, Chelsea, and Frances all in seats by my feet. Everyone looked exhausted and worried, even my dad, although it took me a minute to figure out that the crinkled, tired expression on his face was worry. I hadn't ever seen it before.

"Daddy?" I asked.

He bolted upright. "Cassidy?"

"Daddy!" I squealed, and then, because it sounded good, I sang, "Daddy, daddy, daddy. Daddy, daddy, daddy!" Then I stopped. I hadn't called my father that in, what, five, six years?

"Cassidy. Oh, God, I am so glad that you're okay," Dad sighed, running a hand through his thinning hair. "How are you feeling?"

"I don't know," I said, which was true. "I don't know *what* I'm feeling. Everything . . . everything in my brain feels . . . I don't know, weird. Like . . . foggy, somehow."

"The doctors say that your disease has caught up to you," Dad said, "and I don't want to believe that, really, I don't, but . . . " He trailed off, and I knew what he was thinking.

I reached for his hand, and he let me hold it. It was pale and slightly hairy, but it was warm.

"Dad," I said, "are you real?"

Dad frowned. "'Course I am. Why?"

"Because of the way you've treated me over the years," I said. "You've been dismissive of me. Neglectful. You hardly ever talk, and when you do, it's usually laced with profanity. This all seems like a dream."

Dad ran his thumb over my hand. "Cassidy," he said to me, "I assure you, this is all real. And I'm truly sorry for everything. It's just . . . when you were diagnosed, me and your mom, we kind of panicked. We didn't know how to deal with a kid with a mental illness. And now, when I look back on it, I'm ashamed of myself. Your mom has realized this too. She also has an apology to make."

"Well, finally," I said. I sat up in bed, played an air guitar, and yodeled, "Finally, finally, finally, my parents have come to their senses!" Then I lay back down, laughing.

"Cassidy," said Dad suddenly, "do you want to meet the baby?"

"Are you kidding?" I said. "Of *course,* I want to meet them! But first, I want to see Paco, my Pac-Man, my best friend."

"Of course," Dad said. He got up and went out of the room. I could faintly hear him talking with some nurses, and I closed my eyes, feeling very, very weary all of a sudden.

"Cassidy?" A voice with a Polish accent—*Mr. Watts,* a tiny voice in the back of my head supplied—said. "Cassidy, wake up. Paco's here."

I opened my eyes to find Paco standing next to my bed, a nurse supporting him. I smiled at him. "Hi, Pac-Man!"

"Pac-Man?" Paco said. "Only Alfie calls me that."

I glanced at the other adults in the room, and imagined what they were thinking: *Who the heck is Alfie?!*

"I know," I giggled. "But suddenly, I like the sound of it very much." I looked at Pac-Man's face. He looked terrible.

"The doctors say you're gonna die soon," Paco said, his voice wavering a bit.

"Yup, I probably am," I said and laughed again. For some reason, I found my impending doom to be very funny.

Paco swallowed. "Cass, I don't want you to die."

"Well, you know, as the great Marcus Aurelius (also known as Alfie) said about a couple hundred thousand times in that book he wrote," I said, "all living things must eventually die. And wait, *Cass?*"

"You give me a nickname; I give you a nickname."

I grinned. "*There's* my Paco!"

"Yeah, but seriously, Cassidy, I really don't want you to die," said Paco. "I just got to know you pretty well, and we've only been friends for a few days now, and—and you're one of the only friends I've ever had in my life."

I fell silent. The fog in my mind grew thicker, and I knew I was going to die soon. Soon, as in like thirty minutes. I had a lot of things to do in that time.

"Dad," I said, "I want to see the baby now. Please."

Dad nodded, rose from his chair, spoke to the nurse helping Paco stand up, and sat down again.

The nurse carefully eased Paco into a chair and left.

I leaned back against my pillow, and with nothing else to do, I began planning my home in the Ghost Realm. My own little bungalow on a hill surrounded by a forest of trees, with a porch where I could stare at the starry sky at night, and a tire swing on one of the trees. A picture of Snoopy on his red dog house in my bedroom. A journal full of blank paper, where I could draw even though I wasn't exactly awesome at drawing. I was looking forward to it.

I was disturbed from my little daydream by the sound of a hospital bed being rolled into my room, and the sound of a baby crying. A few nurses, including the one from earlier, pushed the bed up next to mine, and suddenly I was staring into the green eyes of my mother, who was propped up with several pillows. One of the nurses handed Mom a baby, which she kissed on the forehead.

Still cradling the baby, Mom looked directly at me and said simply, "I'm sorry."

"Apology accepted," I said. I had not heard her use the word "I" in so long that it was rather startling to hear it come from her mouth.

Mom smiled and reached across her bed to grasp my hand. Her bleached blond hair, which had once been the same color as mine, before she had dyed it, was loose and tangled, spilling across her shoulders like a chemically-treated waterfall. She was dressed in a blue teddy bear-patterned hospital gown, and she looked quite tired. No wonder; she had just given birth, after all. Right now, she didn't seem devastatingly beautiful as was the case when her face was caked with makeup as it usually was. No, at this moment, she seemed older than she really was, and her face was makeup-free. "Thank you, Cassidy. I love you."

And those simple words, those three, wonderful, wonderful words, made the fog in my mind lift. And suddenly, everything was clear.

"Mom," I said, "can I see the baby?"

"Yes, you may," she said and passed them over to me. "Hold her this way," she instructed, and I copied her.

"So it's a girl?" I asked, looking down on the sweet face of the baby in my arms. She had the brightest blue eyes I'd ever seen, and a tuft of golden-brown hair on her head. She'd stopped crying, and as we gazed at each other, she cooed at me, and I laughed. She reached up and grabbed a lock of my hair, tugging slightly but not enough to hurt.

Mom nodded. "Yep. It was a little hard to figure out her gender since she's intersex—she doesn't have any reproductive organs at all—so we just guessed."

"Cool," I said. The baby let go of my hair and stuck her thumb in her mouth, sucking on it. A little glob of snot dangled from her left nostril, hanging by a thread of gooey mucus. "What's her name?"

"She doesn't have one yet," Mom said. "Would you like to name her?"

I felt the weight of this responsibility and was honored that my parents had trusted me with it. What a difference a baby and a near-death experience make. I pondered the baby for a moment. "Eda," I said finally.

"Eda?" Mom said.

"A cross between Eva and Ada," I responded. "*Ada* after the brilliant mathematician, and *Eva* after a girl I once knew back in preschool."

"Well, I think that's a fine name," Dad cut in. "Don't you think so? It has a certain ring to it: Eda Weldon."

"It's true," Mom agreed. "Eda Weldon *is* a great name."

Mr. Watts, Frances, and Chelsea all murmured their agreement.

"Then it's decided," said Mom. "Eda Weldon it is."

After she'd declared the baby's name, the fog settled again, and I found myself singing *Eda* to the tune of "Old MacDonald." My vision grew fuzzy at the corners of my eyes, and the ever-present smell of almonds grew stronger. I hurriedly gave Eda back to my mother so I wouldn't drop her. My limbs tingled, and my thoughts all blended into a single continuous sentence:

Eda Eda Eda Eda wonder what death'll be like wonder if I'll see Greg again he's handsome what will happen to Mr. Watts and the rest of the staff after I'm gone will they be fired Hope I'll see X again maybe I'll start a book club with J.R.R.Tolkien...

And then all went black.

CHAPTER
EIGHT

Alfie was wrong.

I *did* experience a fluttery sensation in my abdomen, but he'd forgotten to mention the gut-wrenching pain that flared up. But then Beethoven's "Für Elise" started playing, the world lit up, and the pain went away. Then there was a sucking noise, like somebody planting a wet kiss on your cheek, and I felt extremely lightweight. My detached spirit rose a couple of feet before I looked down at my dead green-haired body, and then I floated the rest of the way to the Ghost Realm.

I opened my eyes and found myself standing in front of the same desk I'd stood in front of a few weeks before, when I had been a "guest." I was now just as gray as everybody else. Behind the desk, Greg's handsome face smiled at me. This time his suit was checkered black-and-white, but otherwise, he looked just the same.

"Hello, Miss," said Greg.

"Hey, Greg," I said.

Greg pointed to a tablet on the desk. "If you'll just sign here, Miss."

I signed the tablet with my finger and then waited patiently as Greg did something on his computer.

"Your name is Cassidy Weldon, correct?" Greg asked.

"Yes."

"Age thirteen, female, green hair, creepy makeup, short?" said Greg.

"Yep, that's me."

"Excellent." Greg glanced at his computer again, then said, "You're to be put in your own private bungalow called Half Moon House, Ash Lane, Heaven."

"Sounds good," I said. "Wait, hold up—did you just say Heaven? As in *the* Heaven?"

"There's only one Heaven, miss," Greg said.

I was astonished. "But—but *why?* I don't deserve to be in Heaven! I've done tons of bad stuff, like pranking my mom and drawing horns and evil grins on pictures of my parents with permanent marker!"

"Well, apparently, delivering Miss Gertrud to where she belongs made up for all that," said Greg. He pointed at an escalator going down in the far corner of the room, where a guard stood (presumably to keep the wrong people from entering Heaven). "That's the Stairway to Heaven there. You have a map of Heaven as well as a map of the Ghost Realm in your pocket because ghosts belonging in Heaven are free to go to the Ghost Realm whenever they please, and one thousand gold coins, which is Heaven's currency."

I put my hand in my pocket, and sure enough, I felt two folded-up pieces of paper and a bunch of coins. "One last thing. Why does the stairway to Heaven go down?"

"Oh, that's because Heaven is deep below the surface of Earth's crust," Greg said. "What, did you think that Heaven was in the sky? The mortals' belief that Heaven is in the sky always cracks me up. It's under Earth's surface. Duh."

I pondered that for a minute and decided, given the laws of the universe, Heaven underground sounded much cozier. "Right," I said. "So Hell is in the sky, then?"

"Wow, you catch on quickly," said Greg. "Anyway, terribly sorry to interrupt this pleasant conversation, but other souls are waiting to be checked in."

"Oh, sorry," I said. "I'll go right away."

"Welcome back, Miss Cassidy," said Greg, and called out, "Next!"

PART TWO

CHAPTER
NINE

E da Weldon, twenty years later:
I had just returned my hair to its typical color, a bright green that I had chosen seventeen years ago to honor my sister, Cassidy. In the pictures I'd studied of her, she'd always had green hair, and while hers was kind of wild and mine was the carefully coiffed style of a very successful business owner who had a certain reputation to maintain, I loved that I paid homage to her with my hair.

But it wasn't only my hair that tied me to Cass. We had two other special connections, too. First, her best friend Paco was the man I called Uncle Pac-Man. He had been helping me out ever since I was born, my mom and dad said. Apparently, he was the first person to give me a taste of chocolate, and for that alone, I would forever be grateful. But he also funded my college education, helped set me up in my first apartment, and checked in every week to see how my business was going.

And that's the second way I kept connected to my sister. I'd started a business called Charon Enterprises. We helped both living and dead people cross to the Realm of Ghosts on either a temporary or permanent basis as needs required. Cassidy was our liaison in the Realm, and when we had that rare customer who made it into Heaven, where Cass herself resided, my sister gave them the VIP treatment and helped them get established in the world, just like Uncle Pac-Man had done for me.

Today, though, was extra special because I was making my own quinquennial visit to the Realm to spend a day with Cassidy. I didn't get to go often, given the risks involved with going into a coma, but Alfie had assured me that visiting once every five years would do no permanent damage. Of course, I wanted to go more often, but I'd had to settle for our inter-world video chats most of the time. At least we could email and text and video chat, though.

Now, though, Pac-Man, Alfie, and I were in my sister's childhood room, which Mom and Dad had turned into a sort of Ghost Realm Interface space as an alternative to those really sad shrines parents often made to their dead kids. Her stuff was still there, but they'd also added two large video screens for chats, four comfy beds for those making visits, and a candle of epic proportions—we're talking the size of a refrigerator—for calling in ghosts who were being a little more resistant to making the transition or to guide those who were lost in our world to us. They'd also installed a fountain that served Sprite on demand for just that purpose as well.

"Eda, lay down now, child," Alfie said. He'd always called me child, and I kind of liked it, still. "Think of pleasant things."

Since this was my third trip, I didn't need much more guidance as I let my mind flit from one thing to another: alpacas, my sister's wild eyeshadow, peanut-butter-and-banana sandwiches, the smell of leaves on a sunny autumn day . . .

When I felt alert again, I found myself at the front gate of Heaven, and my sister's husband, Greg, was staffing the desk as usual. He'd been in the Ghost Realm a while longer than

Cass, but since people could decide to be whatever age they wanted here, Cass had quickly made herself twenty-four, and after they had gotten to know one another for a while, they'd gotten married. He'd given up his ultra-modern apartment and gotten a special dispensation from the powers that be to live in her bungalow in Heaven. They seemed quite happy.

Greg stood up. "Good to see you, sis," he said and gave me a hug.

"You, too, bruh," I said even though I hated calling Greg that. He insisted the nickname made him feel cool, and it really was the least I could do.

I looked around, hoping to see my sister. "Cass working?"

"Nope, no way, Eda," a voice said from behind me. "I was just grabbing these." She held up a bag of stroopwafels, and my mouth immediately started watering.

"My favorite," I said as I hugged my sister and tried to grab the bag of crunchy, chewy goodies from her. "You remembered?"

"Seriously, you thought I'd forget when you had a bag carefully placed next to you on your desk the last time we chatted?" She rolled her eyes and then kissed Greg on the cheek. "See you later," she said and dragged me across the lobby to Heaven's escalator.

"Thanks, Hubert," she said as the very large man who guarded the entrance to Heaven pushed the down button for her. "Looking good."

"Thanks, Ms. Weldon," Hubert said in a voice so quiet it was almost a whisper. Apparently, Hubert could break a person's arm with two fingers, but he was also the caretaker of a large collection of bonsai trees and stray kittens that had, since Cass's arrival, begun making their way into the Ghost Realm.

Cass and Greg swore they had nothing to do with the

change in the Ghost Realm's animal policy in the past twenty years, but given the cans of cat food I found stored in their pantry on my last visit, I thought they might just be giving me plausible deniability as a precaution against the powers that be.

"Now," Cass said as the elevator door closed, "what do you want to do? We have a new cloud-jumping course if you're interested in doing something active. Or we could go see a movie. Chadwick Boseman has done a whole new Heaven-based take on *Black Panther*, and I hear it's superb." She flicked her wild green hair over her shoulder.

"Actually, could we just hang out? Maybe sit on your porch and listen to Metallica or something?" Cass had introduced me to the band years ago, but it was hard to find them on Earth now since they weren't just classic rock anymore, but sort of a new form of classical music. I couldn't stand going from Beethoven to AC/DC directly.

Cass smiled. "I love that idea. Peanut-butter-and-banana sandwiches, stroopwafels, and what is it now—root beer or cream soda?"

I laughed. "Strawberry lemonade," I said. I had a habit of becoming absolutely transfixed with a particular drink for a few months at a time. Lately, my cravings had been for strawberry lemonade. We settled into Cass's porch with blankets over our laps and cups of the strawberry lemonade that just appeared at Cass's simple wish in our hands. I was crunching away at my first stroopwafel of the afternoon when she asked the first question she always asked, "How are Mom and Dad?"

"Oh, you know," I said. "Same as ever, really, except that Mom decided to lose her beehive hairdo."

Cassidy chuckled. "What's her preferred look now?"

"A perm with the ends dyed bright pink," I told her.

At this, she threw back her head and laughed in the loud,

happy way she always did. "Seriously?" Cassidy asked, wiping at her eyes with the sleeve of her sweater.

"Seriously. I couldn't even make up stuff like that."

Cassidy grinned again, her blue eyes sparkling with silent laughter. "Yeah, I doubt I could either. Anyway, how's Layla?"

I'd started dating a gal named Layla a few years back, and we'd become inseparable after our first date. Layla didn't usually join me in visiting my sister, though, because she claimed it made her tummy turn. I seriously doubted that, though; Layla might as well have been made of steel. I theorized that being surrounded by dead people just freaked her out. With her petite frame, soft brown eyes, silky black hair, and job in a salon, she seemed like a meek, quiet girl. But she was really as fierce as a dragon. Once, she'd actually challenged a random dude to a fistfight. He had wisely declined. The only thing she was really scared of besides heights was ghosts.

"She's doing great, too," I said. "Recently, she started wearing these freaky clothes from way back when you were alive."

"Oh, yeah, those," said Cassidy. "Mom used to love those. Me, not so much."

"They show off her belly, which is weird because no one I know—other than Layla, of course—goes around with their stomachs exposed. But, you know, they actually look pretty good on her even though they're super weird," I said.

"Crop tops used to be in style when I was alive, actually," Cassidy said. "I wonder how people progressed from extremely revealing clothing to plain T-shirts, baggy pants, stud earrings, and combat boots."

I shrugged. "I dunno. People are weird." I reached for my second stroopwafel and shoved it into my mouth, then washed it down with a swig of strawberry lemonade.

"True that," Cassidy agreed. She raised her cup of

lemonade and shouted, "To the eternal weirdness of human beings!"

"To the eternal weirdness of human beings," I echoed, raising my glass and clinking it against hers.

We both laughed and turned to watch the sky turn from blue to orange, pink, red, and purple, then to deep blue. Stars dotted it like freckles dotted Layla's fair face, and the interesting thing was, they were arranged in constellations that didn't exist on Earth. Every time I visited my sister, the constellations were always different. Tonight, there was a constellation of a jack-o'-lantern, a pod of dolphins, Mickey Mouse, Winnie the Pooh, and the words Go Kansas City Chiefs!

I finished my lemonade and stroopwafels, then tossed off the heavy woolen blanket that lay on my lap. I stood up and stretched, then said to Cassidy, "Want to swing on the tire swing?"

Cass grinned. "You bet. Go on ahead; I'll be right behind you."

I let out a Peter-Pan-style whoop and jumped over the railing of the porch. It was on the second floor of Cassidy's little bungalow, but Heaven was designed so it was just about impossible for someone to get hurt, and apparently, that included the living.

I landed lightly on my feet, turned, and waved at my sister. She waved back and motioned for me to go on. I did, running to the tire tree at the edge of the forest.

I watched as Cassidy launched herself off of the porch railing. She fell at breakneck speed until a magical wind swooped in and slowed her descent. She landed on all fours—like a cat —and bowed to a pretend audience. "Thank you, thank you, really, it was nothing big, so glad you came, thank you!"

Cassidy then ran over to where I stood. Looking up at me—

I was at least a couple of inches taller than her—she said, "So, who wants to go first?"

"Me," I said.

"Knew you'd say that." Cassidy tied her hair with a scrunchy so it wouldn't interfere, then helped me clamber onto the tire. Grabbing two of the three chains that attached the tire to the tree, she pulled it back, then pushed it forward, back, forward, back, forward, gaining momentum, and then with her incredible strength (she'd obviously been working out at Heaven's gym) spun the tire around.

I shrieked with laughter as the tire climbed high into the air, spinning so fast that the whole world became a blur.

Just as I'd begun to swing, I thought I heard X calling to Cass, and when I'd looked at her, her expression was, well, scared. She looked terrified, but not in the kind of way that she might be if X were a serial killer or something. More like in the way someone looked when they had a secret they didn't want to tell.

I couldn't tell what was going, and I didn't have a chance to ask because I woke up back in Cassidy's room. I know, it's lame, a silly cliché from the worst of the worst stories in the world, but it's the truth. Cass's newfound strength spun me right back to consciousness, which I was half-convinced had been intentional.

All this flitted through my mind in the seconds after I opened my eyes to find Uncle Pac-Man snoozing and Alfie playing what looked like Candy Crush on his cellphone. He'd been a ghost long enough to start interacting with technology, and mindless games on his phone were now how he spent most of his time. I couldn't say I blamed him. He'd been around a long time. Checking out for a while seemed completely reasonable.

I quickly ran over to the computer and dialed Cass's

number over in Heaven. She didn't pick up, which was weird since I knew she was at home. I mean, she could have scooted off somewhere right away after I left, but the only reason she would have done that was to avoid me calling, which she could just do by not answering the computer. So my bets were on the fact that she was home and avoiding me.

"I need to go back in," I shouted, starting Pac-Man awake that he jerked up so suddenly that the string of drool from his mouth flung across Alfie's computer screen, which was the way he chose to interact with us when showing up in "person" took too much effort on his part. I thought of it as being like preferring to text instead of talk on the phone. "Now!"

Alfie looked up and blinked a few times. "What, child? No, you cannot. It's too dangerous."

"He's right," Pac-Man said as he rubbed sleep from his left eye. "You know that."

I stared at these two men I loved and who I knew loved me, and then I lay down and willed myself back into the Ghost Realm. I felt myself floating away, and I knew I was almost there when BAM! It felt like a door slammed in my face, and I was wide awake again with a blazing headache. "What. Was. That?!" I shouted.

"Okay, stop with all the shouting," Pac-Man said. "You're giving me a headache."

"YOU have a headache," I shouted, but a little more quietly this time. "My head feels like someone is exploring it with a very pointy toothpick." I put my hand to my head and rubbed, which was no help at all.

Alfie shook his head. "I told you, returning is dangerous. You might not find it as easy to come out of the coma—"

I interrupted him. "No, you don't understand. I didn't make it in this time." I shook my head. "It's like the realm is closed," I explained what had just happened, but they didn't believe me.

"Maybe your body just resisted?" Pac-Man asked.

I shook my head.

"Yeah, that's probably it," Alfie added.

"No, that's not it," I said. "I'll show you."

I laid down on the floor again and let myself drift off. WHACK! I was back but with an even bigger headache. "See?"

"It did look like you drifted away," Pac-Man said. "Let me try." He put himself in position, and within a few moments, his body had gone completely slack, a sure sign he was in a coma. Unlike me, though, he didn't slam back into his body immediately.

Instead, it took another fifteen or so minutes for him to return, and when he did, he was shifty. He'd been doing this trip for decades now, and he was more practiced at it. Normally, though, he was a strange combination of content and sad. Now, though, he was definitely hiding something. I could tell by the way he wouldn't meet my eyes.

When I asked him what happened, he told me had a normal visit, "a nice chat with Greg. Nothing unusual or weird or strange at all."

See? Shifty. He wasn't telling me something, and I wanted to know what it was. So I tried all my best tricks to get him to do what I wanted. Every single one of them involved food, and to enact them, I had to raid Mom and Dad's pantry, a task I could not undertake alone.

"Whatever it is you want me to do," said Layla, "yes."

I blinked. "I didn't even ask you anything."

"Yeah, but you had that look on your face."

"What look?"

"You know, the one where you stare at me with those beautiful, soulful, enchanting sapphire eyes of yours with this whacked-up expression like you just ate a lemon," said Layla.

"It could have been love," I said.

"Coulda, because I know that I'm the most lovable person on the face of this Earth, but I know you, Eda, and that was not love. No, that was most certainly something else entirely," Layla concluded.

"Wow, great job, Sherlock," I said.

Layla flipped her hair, sending a wave of citrus-smelling air into my face. "Actually, I prefer Nancy Drew."

We sat on a bench at the park, watching dogs chasing after balls thrown by their owners and toddlers playing on the swings. It was lunchtime, and we had just finished munching on our sandwiches—mine, cream cheese and grape jelly, Layla's, peanut butter and marshmallow. Layla wore a white crop top that had the words "California Gurls" (even though it was literally in the forties outside) printed in pink across it, a baggy pair of heated black pants, zero-gravity combat boots with removable weights, and her usual good looks. Me, I just wore what everybody else wore: a plain T-shirt, shorts with pockets that allowed you to pull out just about anything you could want, and shoes that had two settings: normal and seven-league, for those who wanted to take giant steps with minimal effort.

"So," said Layla, "as I was saying before you so rudely interrupted me, yes, I accept whatever you want me to do."

"Because you're my girlfriend and that's exactly what couples always do in the movies?" I asked.

"Yeah."

I laughed and put my arm around her shoulder. "All right, here's what I need you to do. You know Mom and Dad's pantry, right?"

Mom and Dad were possibly some of the only people who had a pantry in our town. Years ago, they had been quite common, but then some scientist guy came up with what she called the UltraFridgerator™, which let you put everything into it. There was the normal refrigerator part, and then there was a part that looked like a wooden refrigerator sliced in half, where all your non-refrigerated stuff went. We had one of those things, but my parents had insisted upon keeping the old pantry due to the fact that it was, and I quote, "charming and cozy, plus we just like it there." They forgot to mention that it was now utterly useless thanks to the UltraFrigerator™. So whenever Dad or Mom went shopping, they bought twice the amount of groceries they needed so they could fill said pantry to make it look like it wasn't useless. Great job with that, Mom and Dad. Fortunately for me, that meant they would probably not miss it if everything in it suddenly vanished.

Now, I know you're dying to know the plan, but I'm not going to tell you, not if you offer me a hundred metal pieces (Earth's current currency) and ten bags of Swedish fish.

You say you'll give me two hundred metal pieces and two family-sized bags of Swedish fish? Hmm. Okay, I'll give it some thought.

Oh, all right. I'll tell you.

THE PLAN:

1. Raid parents' pantry and get all of the coffee beans available.
2. Get Layla to distract Alfie and Uncle Pac-Man with the story of how she broke her arm when attempting to juggle ten full cartons of milk on roller skates (I sincerely apologize for doing this to you, Alfie and Pac-Man).
3. Go to childhood bedroom.
4. Light candles in a star shape around me and my bed, then place a bag of coffee beans at each tip of

the star.

5. Attempt to fall into coma.

The first step went pretty well. Since my parents both loved coffee—Dad preferred dark roast, while Mom liked decaf better—about half of the pantry was overflowing with various bags of coffee, and I was able to help myself. Thank goodness for huge duffel bags.

The second step was a little more difficult. My old room was right across from Cass's, so Pac-Man and Alfie could see me if they looked hard enough at the right angle. I closed the door, though, so that solved any problems I might've had. I could faintly hear Layla narrating loudly, and I smiled to myself. All was going well.

I completed the other steps, then slipped into unconsciousness.

Ghosts, as I had discovered many years ago, were quite fond of coffee. I didn't know why. But when Sprite and refrigerator-sized candles failed, coffee was sure to succeed. I was hoping that with coffee beans surrounding me, I would be allowed to go into the Ghost Realm.

I opened my eyes, and my heart did a little victory dance. It had worked. I stood in front of the now-familiar desk. Greg wasn't there. Instead, there was a person with short brown hair, an angular face, considerable height, and dark eyes staring at me from behind a pair of round black-rimmed glasses. Their name tag read *Art*♥.

"You're not supposed to be here," said Art.

"Huh?" I said, confused.

"Cassidy specifically said, 'Do not let my sister Eda in,'" Art said, pushing their glasses further up their nose. "She gave a precise description of you: A young woman with a height of exactly five foot eight, green hair of the exact same shade as hers with golden brown roots, slightly tan arms, a British accent from the time that you lived in London."

"Why would Cassidy prevent me from entering the Ghost Realm?" I asked.

Art shrugged. "I don't know. She just told me to do it."

"And who are you, exactly?" I said.

"I'm X's friend, who is Cassidy's friend, so therefore I am her friend," said Art. "Besides, I owed her. She helped me get my bearings in this place."

I sighed. "Well, this trip has been a flop."

"I'm sorry to hear that," Art said in their flat voice.

"Mm-hmm," I said. "Okay, I'm gonna go now, but would you mind sending a message to my sister for me?"

"Sure," they said, rubbing their pointer finger and thumb together and looking at me hopefully.

"No, I'm not giving you a tip," I said. "I don't have any joss paper on me right now."

Art deflated. "Aw."

"Okay, here's my message," I said. "What the heck is going on!"

"That's the message you want me to deliver?" Art asked.

"Yup," I said.

"Okay, I'll tell her that, but I'm not really a very loud sort of person, so I won't be quite as ear-splitting as you. But I'll try my best," Art said.

"Goodbye," I said and woke up.

When I returned to my bed, the candles were blown out, and Layla was leaning over me with a worried expression. Behind her, Pac-Man stood with Alfie's computer so they could both shoot daggers at me.

"Hi," I said.

"Hi," said Layla.

I tried to sit up, but Layla was sitting on top of me, so I

couldn't. "Layla," I said, "please get off of me."

Layla slid off of the bed and stood up.

"Thank you," I said. I sat up and turned to Pac-Man and Alfie. "Guys, why are you glaring at me like that?"

"Because you went into a coma without permission or supervision, and you got your girlfriend to distract us while you did it!" Pac-Man yelled. "Can you even fathom how dangerous that is? Did you actually even consider the possibility that you may not have woken up! Just look at Cassidy! The first and only time she went into a coma, she almost didn't wake up! Jesus!"

"And," Alfie shouted, "you didn't even consult us! Eda, that was unbelievably stupid! You're lucky you woke up!"

I looked down, suddenly interested in the patchwork of my old quilt. "Sorry."

Layla turned to Pac-Man and Alfie and said, "Guys! GUYS! Shut up for one moment, will you?"

The whole room suddenly fell silent, ashamed.

Layla took a deep breath and said, "Alfie and Paco, I apologize for helping Eda with this plot that, now that you mention it, was very risky. And I'm sure that Eda is also very sorry. But you don't have to scream at her like that. Besides, Eda had no idea what was going on with her sister and her blocked entrance to the Ghost Realm. It's natural for her to try to figure out what was happening. So, in short, we should all be ashamed of ourselves."

"Sorry, Eda," said Alfie humbly.

"Yeah," Pac-Man chimed in. "Me too."

"I'm sorry, too," I said. "It didn't even work. I couldn't get past the front desk." I sighed heavily.

Awkward silence reigned in the room for a bit before I said, a bit gloomily, "I guess I should go put these coffee bags back, huh?"

They all nodded.

I began picking up the coffee, with Layla assisting me. Pac-Man and Alfie left, and we went downstairs to put the coffee bags back.

As we stuffed the coffee back into the pantry, I said to Layla, "Thanks for standing up for me back there."

"No problem," said Layla. "But, you know, they did have a point. That was a very dangerous thing for you to do. I mean, I know I do dangerous things all the time, like doing wheelies on motorcycles made thirty years ago, but this was actually life-threatening."

"I know," I said quietly. "I just—I just—"

"Eda," Layla said gently. "It's okay. You woke up, and you're still alive—hooray!—so that's all that matters right now."

"Okay," I said. We finished shoving the coffee bags in the pantry, kissed, and then she went back home to babysit her little brother's son.

I went into the living room and watched an episode of *Charmed*. Most of me was distracted by what was going on in the show, but part of my mind kept straying to my little run-in with Art. Why didn't Cassidy want me in the Ghost Realm? I knew my occasional visit was over, and I wasn't allowed to do it more often than once every five years, but now it seemed as if she really, really, *really* didn't want me stopping by every few years.

Wow, my brain hurt.

When *Charmed* was over, I turned the TV off and sat pondering.

I climbed the stairs to Cassidy's bedroom and sat on one of the four beds in there. Alfie's computer was back in its usual spot on the table next to the entrance, and it was blank, so I knew he was sleeping.

I didn't want to disturb him, but I really had to talk to him.

Weird things were going on, and I had no idea what was happening.

I took a breath and tapped on the screen. "Alfie?" I asked.

Alfie's bearded, sideburned face popped into view, yawning and stretching. "Eda? Goodness, child, I was sleeping! As if today needs any more drama."

"Sorry to wake you up, Alfie," I said. "I really need to talk to you."

"Why? What's wrong? Who died?" Alfie said, suddenly awake.

"No one died, Alfie," I said. "It's just . . . Cass won't reach out to me. I haven't received a single text from her in hours, and we usually chat for a bit every day. I'm worried about her. Like, really, *really* worried. And during my visit to her earlier, I was on the swing before I woke up, and I heard somebody—X, I think—yelling something to her, and she looked really, really scared. Like the kind of fear you have when we're keeping secrets."

Alfie nodded. "Yes, I daresay we've all had our share of *those*, even me, and I'm generally remembered as being the most amazing, philosophical, purest dude ever."

"Which you're not," I said.

"Correct. History seems to have forgotten that I missed my grandfather's birthday feast, and I accidentally ruined my best buddy's buddy Petrus's brand-new red-trimmed toga when I spilled that platter of chicken roasted in wine on a bed of fresh lettuce soaked in a salad dressing of olive oil," Alfie sighed. "Ah, yes, I remember that moment like it was yesterday. How Petrus shrieked! That was his favorite toga, as I recall. He was really sad. I felt awful after that incident."

"I'll bet," I said sympathetically. Since we were veering from the main subject, I quickly corrected our course and said, "So, about Cassidy . . . "

"Oh! Cassidy!" Alfie slapped his forehead. "Goodness gracious, I forgot about that! Thanks for reminding me. Well, Eda, it seems like you've got yourself stuck in a bit of a pickle."

"That would be correct," I said. "I just don't know what's going on. This has never happened before. I can't remember doing anything wrong to her. Maybe it was the stroopwafels?"

"No. NO. Never, Eda. Never consider that possibility. Stroopwafels are among the greatest things in the world, right next to water buffalo, kangaroos, French fashion, Canada, and the Internet. No, I am most certain that whatever is causing this problem, it is not the stroopwafels. Now, what you need, child, is a bit of relaxing Tibetan meditation music," Alfie announced.

I managed a small smile despite everything that had happened. "Oh, boy." Alfie's go-to was Tibetan meditation music, and while it wasn't my favorite, I did have to admit it was pretty relaxing.

Alfie quickly accessed YouTube and put some music on. The clear, calming sound of gongs began to play, and then my Roman ex-emperor ghost friend proceeded to lead me in a series of very difficult yoga poses that left my limbs sore.

In fact, I was so focused on my asanas that I totally forgot that Alfie had been in the Ghost Realm himself for quite a long moment.

On November 30, it finally snowed.

The town in which I lived was not exactly a place where it snowed often. It could get very cold, but snow was rare, and the inhabitants took advantage of it whenever it did snow.

It wasn't a full-on blizzard, but when it snowed here, it tended to snow a lot. Sometimes the snow could be up to your knees.

I stayed inside in my room, watching the snowflakes fall past the window. I could see our spacious lawn, which was gradually being buried by snow, and lots of trees, planted when I was born. Layla lounged across one of my beanbag chairs, thankfully not in one of those crazy crop tops of hers (instead, she wore a sweatshirt with the insignia of the college she was attending printed on it), her shoes scattered across the floor. We both had mugs of Frances's famous hot chocolate and sipped regularly.

"After it stops snowing, do you want to go out and build a snowwoman?" I asked, clasping my cup with both hands so as to better absorb its warmth.

Layla shook her head, her dark locks flying. "Nah, I think I wanna stay here. It's really pretty after it snows. I don't want to ruin it with footprints. Besides, we both know that we are the worst at building snowwomen."

"True," I laughed. We snuggled together, my face buried in her shoulder even though I was about eight inches taller than she was. "So, you just want to hang out and gorge ourselves on Frances's hot chocolate?"

"Yeah," said Layla. "I mean, that woman is like an angel."

"She is," I agreed. "We're lucky to have her."

Layla smiled, then changed the subject. "Any luck with contacting Cassidy?"

This made my spirits fall immediately. "No," I said glumly. "We've been completely out of touch for almost a week now."

"Aw, man," said Layla. "That must be tough. I wouldn't mind not seeing my brother for the rest of my life if he didn't have such an adorable baby boy, but I know you're really close to Cassidy. I know you only knew her as an alive person for like five minutes, and that was when you were a teeny tiny baby, but still. That really must be hard."

I nodded. "I don't know why this is happening, but whatever it is, I really don't like it. I want to see my sister, whether it's in person or on a SpiritChat call."

Layla hugged me. "Aw, sweetheart. Well, whatever happens, I will always be here right by your side, and I know that is like a super-cliché by now due to the fact that basically all Marvel movies have a line like that somewhere in them, and they appear in several million books and songs, etc., etc., but as of this moment, it is very true."

"How did I get such an amazing girlfriend?" I asked.

She smiled and booped my nose. "You gonna finish that hot chocolate or what?"

I snatched my mug away and drained it. I licked the chocolate mustache from my lips and then showed her the empty mug. "Sorry, nothing left for you."

Layla tackled me, and, laughing, we spent the rest of the evening horsing around.

The next day, I woke to find that the snow had stopped falling. But there was, however, a considerable amount of fresh, untrodden snow, which made for some beautiful scenery when you put a few mountains in the background and a couple of young trees in the foreground. Layla had fallen asleep on the beanbag she liked to call hers.

I threw a sweater over the ratty oversized T-shirt I had slept in and quietly went downstairs. In the kitchen, I heated up some leftover pancakes from yesterday's breakfast, poured chocolate syrup all over it, sprayed whipped cream on it, and carried my plate over to the table in the dining room.

As I ate, I kept checking my phone (in case you're wondering, not a lot of improvements had been made to the cell phone over the past two decades) for any texts, emails, or missed calls from Cass. Nada. I decided that obsessing over the phone was not good for my health, so I put it into my pocket and tried to ignore the urge to dig it out again and check it one more time.

After my lonely breakfast, I went back to my room. Layla was still snoring away, a tiny string of drool (yuck) dangling from the corner of her mouth. I climbed onto her beanbag, laying my long legs over her short ones. Feeling the weight of my body, Layla woke up, wiped away the drool with her sleeve, and stared at me groggily.

"Good morning, Sleeping Beauty," I said to my girlfriend.

"Morning, Princess Charming," Layla replied. "It seems that you have managed to revive me from my eternal sleep. Couldn't you have waited just a few more minutes, though? I was right in the middle of a wonderful dream concerning sheep and Eminem."

"Oops," I said, grinning. "How'd you sleep?"

"Like I said, I was having some pretty good dreams," said Layla. She reached up and ran a hand through her black hair. The fact that it was now tangled somehow made her look even better. "How 'bout you?"

"Oh, you know," I said. "No dreams. I only woke up once to use the bathroom. I'd say it was pretty good."

Layla tucked a stray strand of hair behind my ear. "Glad to hear that, Princess Charming. Now, it seems that you have neglected to give me my true love's kiss."

"Oh, no!" I said, feigning alarm. "I shall fix this grievous error straightaway, my fair lady." Then I kissed her, and for a brief moment, all of my worries and my problems melted away. In that moment, the only person I cared about was Layla.

Layla pulled me closer, her hands sifting through my hair. I kissed her again, pressing against her body, my legs entangling with hers.

Because Frances was calling for us, we stopped.

I ran down the stairs and into the kitchen. "What?"

"Paco wants to see you. He's out on the patio with some other fellow. There's a ghost that needs transporting or such," Frances said. She was in her late fifties, her hair streaked gray and straw-blond, and she was still just as good a cook. She handed me a plate, saying, "Also, can you take these churros to Paco?"

"No problem, Frances," I said.

She smiled and said, "Thanks, darlin'. And I better not catch you sneaking some for yourself!"

I grinned and went onto the patio. It was cold, but I was fairly resistant to temperatures like this, so I was fine. Pac-Man and the other guy that Frances had mentioned sat at the table, decked out in warm clothing. I passed the plate to Pac-Man, who snatched a churro off of it and stuffed it in his mouth. He offered one to the gentleman sitting across from him, and the new guy accepted, eagerly taking a large bite of the warm pastry.

I dragged another chair over to the table and sat. I studied the newcomer for a moment. He had short, curly golden-blond hair, amber eyes, a bit of day-old stubble, and a lanky frame. Under his unzipped coat, he wore a Rolling Stones T-shirt. He must've gotten that shirt from eBay; those weren't very common anymore.

Pac-Man swallowed and began to speak. "Eda, I want you to meet my friend—"

"Boyfriend," the guy corrected.

"—Boyfriend Seamus," Pac-Man finished.

I raised my eyebrow. "Seamus, huh. Isn't that a character from Harry Potter?"

"Yeah, I get that a lot," Seamus chuckled.

"Uncle," I said to Pac-Man, "you never told me you had a boyfriend."

"Well, it only became official a couple of days ago," said Pac-Man shyly. "Besides, I haven't really come out about being bisexual to a lot of people."

"Oh," I said. "Well, that makes sense. Sometimes coming

out can be scary. Take a look at me, for example. I didn't come out as lesbian until just after high school."

Seamus nodded in agreement. "I like this gal already. Plus, the green hair is cool."

"Thank you," I said. "I dyed it in honor of my sister."

"Yeah, I know," said Seamus. "Paco told me all about you. Apparently you're really successful in transporting lost ghosts to the Ghost Realm. You're like the Charon of the whole place, right?"

"Yup," I said. "Been at it for over a decade."

"Seamus is very interested in ghosts and other such paranormal activities," Pac-Man told me. "He is the vice president of the Paranormal Club at the community center and often leads séances."

"Really?" I said to Seamus.

"Yeah. It's kinda just a hobby, not really for anything serious. And the séances are just for fun; they don't usually do anything," said Seamus.

"Do you do Ouija boards?" I asked.

Seamus shook his head. "Nah, that kind of stuff is bogus. And it's also kinda hard to follow along because I'm dyslexic."

"I'm not dyslexic, but it *is* tough for me to use Ouija boards too," I said.

"I'm just liking you better and better, and we just met," Seamus said.

"Same here."

"So, Eda, a few days ago, Seamus found a ghost," Pac-Man said, changing the subject.

I was even more interested. "Really?"

"Well, he didn't actually find a ghost; something just appeared on his radar," Pac-Man clarified. "And he thinks that it's in the basement of our house."

"Do you know who it is?" I asked.

Seamus grinned. "Yup, and you'll never guess who."

"Duke Ellington?" I guessed.

"Close."

"Louis Armstrong?"

"You're getting there. I'm giving you one last shot."

"Mozart?"

"Nope. Sorry. You were in the right category, though."

"Who is it, then?" I queried.

"Wait for it . . . " Seamus made a big show of doing a drum-roll and announced, "It's Count Basie!"

"Count Basie? Count Basie is in the basement of my house?" I asked, wide-eyed.

"Well, Alfie *is* Marcus Aurelius, so I suppose anything's possible," said Pac-Man.

"True," I said. "That is very true."

"So, what're we gonna do now? Go into the basement and have a look around?" Pac-Man asked Seamus.

"Yep. Wow, Paco, you're really great at reading my mind," said Seamus. The two gazed at each other with lovey-dovey looks on their faces until I cleared my throat and reminded them of our task.

We picked up the half-empty plate of churros and went inside. I quickly showed Seamus Cass's old room and allowed him to grab a can of Sprite, and then we went downstairs into the basement.

The basement wasn't that old, cobwebby, cluttered place like you usually see in movies and books. We'd shoved most of our excess stuff into the attic, so the basement was basically empty except for a couple of unopened boxes, garden supplies, and a random tub labeled "Diapers." It was slightly dark, though, because three of the six different lights in the basement had blown out.

"Huh," said Seamus. "Surprisingly un-spooky."

"Yeah, we've never really used it much. When I was ten, I thought there were all sorts of cool things in here because I was —and kind of still am—a total bookworm (and we know basements in books are always full of awesome finds), and also I'd never been down here before. So one day, far later into my life than one might expect, I went into the basement and was, needless to say, severely disappointed," I said.

Seamus took off his backpack and rifled through it, looking for something. Finally, he emerged with a stick of gum and a cell phone. He unwrapped the gum, popped it into his mouth, and began chewing, tapping on his phone for a bit. Finally, he showed us an app that let him track ghosts.

"That's really cool," I said, staring at the screen. There was a map of my entire house, with what I knew was Alfie upstairs in Cassidy's bedroom. I could see his name floating above his head on the map. Then, in the basement, we were shown in neon orange—I squinted—a faint figure in the far corner. Above the figure, there were the words "Count Basie" written in the same color as the ghost was shown.

"I think you're right, Seamus," I said after he'd put his phone away. "There *is* definitely something here, and it *is* Count Basie."

We walked toward the far corner of the room, where Count Basie was supposed to be. Pac-Man looked nervous—I knew he was slightly afraid of ghosts even though he'd been dealing with them for almost his entire life, but hey, I couldn't blame him; some ghosts could be pretty scary. Seamus, however, just looked giddy. I considered hiring him.

As soon as we got close enough, I caught a whiff of almond, and my sharp eyes found a puff of blue. *Yup, definitely a ghost*, I thought. I retrieved two candles from my pocket, and Pac-Man handed me a lighter. I lit the candles, placed them on the floor horizontally, and fished a can of Sprite from the pocket of my sweater. I didn't put the Sprite on the floor; instead, I simply stood between the two candles and held out the Sprite to what appeared to be thin air—to the untrained eye.

I felt a draft of cold air against my hand, and something invisible grabbed the Sprite. I let go of it, and for a few seconds, the soda hovered in the air. Then something popped the tab and raised the can up to its invisible lips. As the ghost drank, it slowly became visible.

By the time the phantom had finished the can of Sprite and tossed it onto the floor, it was fully visible. I could clearly see that it was indeed Count Basie.

The spirit of Count Basie had beautiful dark skin with a grayish tone to it, short salt-and-pepper hair shaved close to his scalp, a receding hairline, a mustache, and a snazzy tuxedo. Count Basie had a slightly unhappy expression, probably because he hadn't touched a piano for so long.

"Boy, that stuff is strong," Count Basie rumbled, letting out a burp.

"Hi, Count Basie," I said. "And the reason why it's strong is probably because of the insane amount of sugar in it. Also, it's carbonated."

"Well, that explains it," Basie said. He pointed a ghostly, well-manicured finger at the empty Sprite can on the floor. "Would you mind throwing that in the recycling bin for me? I'd do it myself, but there's no recycling bin nearby, and I'm afraid that I can't stray from the basement."

"Why can't you leave?" I asked, picking the can up.

"You got a nice basement. Besides, I don't like haunting people. I tried my hand at it once, and I hated it. Never again."

I handed the can to Pac-Man, and he immediately turned and sprinted back upstairs. "Well, Count Basie, how would you feel about going to the Ghost Realm?"

"Oh, that would be fantastic!" Basie said dreamily. "I've

heard about it from Alfred upstairs. I used to chat with him because being a ghost who can only move a few square feet in three different directions without a piano is lonely. As long as I don't run into Duke Ellington, I'd be very happy there."

"Count Basie, you just got very lucky," I said, "because I just happen to be the owner of a business that helps guide lost ghosts to the Ghost Realm. You just have to sign a contract that once you get to the Ghost Realm, you have to pay us back with a thousand bucks' worth of whatever currency you have."

"That seems like a fair deal," Basie said.

"Let me just get my stuff from upstairs, okay?" I said. "I'll only take a minute or so."

"I can wait," said Count Basie. "I've waited over fifty years. I can wait a coupla minutes more."

I dashed upstairs, retrieved more candles, Sprites, and the contract, and ran back to the basement. Pac-Man had just come back from recycling the Sprite can and joined me.

While we walked, I asked, "Uncle, could you guide Count Basie on his journey?"

"Why?" Pac-Man said. "You know I'm scared of ghosts."

"Yeah, but I'm not allowed in the Ghost Realm now, remember?" I explained.

"Oh, that's right," Pac-Man slowed but kept walking and I wondered if he was going to say something important, but he just said, "All right. Just this once, though."

"Thanks, Uncle," I said. He gave me a small smile, and we entered the basement.

With little effort, Pac-Man successfully guided Count Basie to the Ghost Realm, where he settled down in a quiet little neighborhood called Musician's Corner (thankfully, Duke Ellington did not live there). But my uncle also brought a message from Cassidy: "Check your email!"

CHAPTER
TEN

Dear Eda,

I'm sorry that you're worried, but I'm doing it for your own good. The Ghost Realm is disappearing. Ghosts are disappearing. We aren't safe anymore. That's why we're relocating to a nameless place, a place beyond sight and sound, a place between the north and the south, the east and the west. Guests don't go to the Ghost Realm anymore. They just sleep. I'm sorry, Eda. I love you, but I may not see you ever again, even when you die. This might be the last you'll ever hear from me. I love you, Eda. Say hi to Dad and Mom and everyone else too. Everything will be okay. Trust me, Eda. Just trust me. Okay?

Love you, sis,

Cass

A tiny part of me appreciated that Cassidy had sent a note, but mostly, I was just royally mad. Trust her?! How could I trust her when she'd locked me away from seeing her *and* from doing my job without any explanation? And what in the world did I need to be protected from anyway? I wasn't a ghost, so I wasn't going to disappear.

I needed Earl Grey stat. Fortunately, in addition to my parents' massive stash of coffee, they kept an entire shelf of teas, including three kinds of my dad's favorite, Earl Grey. Dad always drank it when he had to think, but I liked the way the flowery taste fueled my anger. My rage tasted like roses.

I closed my computer and then opened it again. I couldn't stop staring at Cassidy's email. What the heck did it mean? I loved my sister, but honestly, sometimes her cryptic messages really irritated me.

I took a break from obsessively glaring at the email and went downstairs, where I selected an Earl Grey tea and brewed myself a mug. Then I went back to my room, where I resumed staring at the message between sips of tea.

Layla had left earlier to babysit her nephew, so I was all alone. Strangely, though, the solitude cleared my mind. I put on some music—not Tibetan healing music (sorry, Alfie)—and, half listening, attempted once again to decipher Cassidy's email, with no success.

One of my favorite songs, "Song of the Sea" by Lisa Hannigan, came on. I stopped rereading the message to listen and suddenly froze.

North and the South. That was what Cass had written. And she knew I liked this song. I kept listening, searching for more clues.

There it was again! "The east and the west." I strained to find more clues as I listened to the rest of the song.

When it ended, I was left staring at the message with a warm mug of tea, the words of the email just as confusing as the first time I'd read it through.

I couldn't sleep that night. The sheep I'd been trying to count had never shown up. A warm glass of milk hadn't worked, and usually, that was all it took to get me snoring. Not even my prized collection of antique lava lamps had helped.

I sat up in bed, turned on the lamp beside my bed, and got my computer. I Googled the lyrics of "The Song of the Sea," but that didn't help. I checked my emails—nothing, except for an offer to lead a séance at some church on Monday. I rubbed my forehead. Technically, brains can't hurt—they don't have nerves—but it sure seemed like my brain was throbbing.

There was a *ding* from my cell phone, and I snatched it off my bedside table, hoping it was a text from Cassidy.

Nope. It was Layla messaging me. I read it through.

> SuperAwesomeHotGal: Hey, Eda. Hmm, ya know, maybe I should call you Ed. Short for Eda. Anyway. Can't sleep rite now. Can I come ovr? I won't bother u 2 much, I think. Maybe just little bit.

> GhostCrazyLady: You won't be bothering me. I got myself a pair of earplugs when I was out shopping a few days ago. They work really good. I tried them out on Alfie himself. So, yeah, you can come over. I can't sleep, either.

> SuperAwesomeHotGal: Alrighty! See ya there in, oh, idk, 10 mins, max.

I turned off my phone and lay back down.

Then I got out of bed and went downstairs, as I had drained my whole mug of tea.

I threw the tea bag in the trash, put my mug in the sink, and went to the living room. It was very quiet. I walked over to the window and looked out at the night. The crescent moon illuminated the freshly fallen snow, creating a sort of mystical-looking scene against the darkness of the trees surrounding my house. The stars contrasted sharply against the darkness of the night. As I looked out the window, I felt lonely. I was just a speck in the whole, continually growing, almost never-ending universe. A meaningless thing whose light would be extinguished in the blink of an eye. A tiny guppy in the Pacific Ocean.

I guess I stood there for a long time because then the doorbell rang—it used to have a horrible screech, but it had been fixed years before, so it sounded normal. I knew it was Layla, and I hurried to let her in.

As I fumbled with the doorknob and finally opened the door, a whoosh of cool air swept in, raising goosebumps on my skin.

Layla stood there in a heavy coat that reached her ankles. Knowing her, she'd probably thrown on that coat over her pajamas, and since I knew how intolerant she was to extreme temperatures, I ushered her in immediately.

"Thanks," Layla gasped, yanking off her knit cap and untying the scarf that covered half of her face. "Boy, it's freezing out."

"I know," I said. "I felt it."

Layla looked at me and said, "Nice shirt."

I remembered that I was in nothing but an old, stained shirt that was at least two sizes too big—I think it used to belong to my grandfather—and a pair of flowery underwear, and I flushed. "Uh, thanks. Hey, are those new?" I pointed at the sleeping koala-patterned matching nightshirt and shorts she was wearing, grateful for an excuse to change the subject.

"Yeah, I just bought them a few days ago," said Layla, spinning around so I could see everything. Her nightclothes were form-hugging, accentuating her curvy hips and thighs.

I nodded. "Cool. I like 'em."

"Thanks. I like your old, oversized, paint-stained shirt, especially the guy with tattoos covering his whole arm on the motorcycle on the back of it," said Layla.

"Yeah, Grandpa loved motorcycles."

Layla grinned. "He sounds like a guy I would have liked to meet."

"I don't know what he was really like, actually," I said. "Grandad died before I was born. I never met him. I only know what my parents have told me."

"Aww." Layla frowned. "That's sad."

"So what do you want to do?" I asked.

Layla shrugged. "I dunno. Something fun?"

"How about TV?"

"Sounds good to me," she said. So we went into the living room, turned on some lights, and snuggled up on the couch while an old episode of my sister's favorite TV show *Stranger Things* played. I actually forgot about the weird message from Cassidy for a while, until the ending credits started to roll, and I felt that urge to dig out my computer and look at the email again.

So that's what I did.

I got my computer from upstairs and settled down on the couch again.

Layla noticed it—I was hoping she wouldn't, as watching the ending credits usually hypnotized her—and said, "Why're you on your computer?"

I sighed. "I got a weird email from my sister yesterday. I'm trying to figure it out." I showed it to her.

"Well, staring at it with a blank expression and glazed-over eyes probably isn't gonna help," said Layla after reading the email. "Do you think that if you stare at it for long enough, some magical solution will just pop into your beautiful, very attractive head?"

"Probably not?" I guessed.

"Correct. Start on the road to figuring it out by closing your computer"—Layla pushed the screen down and took it away from me—"and relaxing. Trust me; it'll come eventually."

"How long is *eventually*?" I asked.

"How should I know? Listen, Eda, this kind of thing takes *time*. Time of which you currently have plenty. Try to relax, listen to some Lady Gaga, look up pictures of Drake on your computer, whatever. Anything to take your mind off of this email. This is obviously very stressful for you at the moment, so try to get de-stressed, and all will come in good time," Layla concluded.

"Those last seven words sounded like something from the *Lord of the Rings*," I said.

Layla smiled. "I know, right?"

"So, how do you suggest I forget about this message for the time being?" I asked. "I've tried a lot of things, believe me— even Earl Grey tea."

Layla gasped. "Even Earl Grey? Then this has become a most dire situation, and I can think of only one solution."

"And that is . . ."

Instead of answering me, Layla wrapped her arms around my neck and brought her lips to mine.

Instantly, I felt a rush of exhilaration. I clutched her waist as her weight sent us sprawling backward on the couch. My hair was in disarray, scattered all around my head like a big green uneven halo. My cheeks were cupped in Layla's hands as she kissed me. I wrapped my legs around hers and kissed her back, my lips sliding from hers down to her neck. I made tiny gasping noises as her hands went up the back of my shirt, resting on my skin.

Finally, we pulled away, both of us red-faced and panting. "Did that help?" Layla asked.

I couldn't lie. "Yeah. It did." While I was kissing Layla, there was literally nothing else in my mind. I was focused on her and only her. "Thanks."

"My pleasure," said Layla smoothly. Then we looked at each other, and for some unknown reason, we both started laughing.

"Why are we laughing?" I managed, my chest heaving.

Layla shook her head. "I have literally zero idea."

Still laughing, we kissed again, and my mind was empty except for thoughts of Layla. My hands combed through her dark hair, and her arms might as well have been glued around my neck as our mouths slid together again and again.

Cassidy never popped into my mind during the rest of the night.

Slowly, we made our way up the stairs, still kissing, and went into my room. We collapsed onto one of the beanbags and fell asleep there.

The next morning, I woke up entangled in Layla's arms, my shirt on backwards (I had no idea how it'd gotten that way) and my head resting on her chest. I wiped a small string of drool from my mouth with my sleeve, corrected the position of my shirt, and sat up straight, rubbing the sleep from my eyes. Layla was still sleeping—I swear, that girl could sleep through anything—and snoring quietly. I rolled my shoulders and winced as my muscles cried out in pain. I had slept in a weird position. My limbs would be sore for days now.

Not wanting to wake Layla, because she got *really* grumpy

whenever someone woke her up before she was ready, I put on pants and crept downstairs. Pots and pans clanged in the kitchen, and I thereby concluded that Frances was here. I'd slept past my usual wake-up time; Frances never got here until around eight.

I went into the kitchen, and sure enough, there my old friend was, whipping up a batch of what looked like blueberry pancakes.

"'Morning, Frances," I called.

"Hey, Eda! Good mornin' to you, as well!" Frances said cheerfully. Even after all the years I had known her, her strong Texas accent never seemed to fade. She dropped her spatula and spread her arms wide. "Come on and give me a hug!"

I grinned and went in for the hug, wrapping my arms around her. Frances was about the same height as my sister, so naturally, because I had inherited my father's height, I towered over her. "Are you making blueberry pancakes?"

"Well, clearly, I'm making *some* kind of pancakes," said Frances, flipping one over. "Yes, Eda, I am making blueberry pancakes. Can you guess the secret ingredient?"

"Cinnamon?" I tried.

"Bingo!" Frances said, giving me a thumbs-up. "Actually, it's a mixture of cinnamon and cardamom, so you're partially correct."

"Can't wait to try it," I said. I went over to the coffee maker and made myself a strong cup. I sat myself down on the couch in the living room, which was right across the hall from the kitchen. The pillows and blankets were in disarray from last night, and I tidied up a bit while I sipped my coffee and waited for breakfast.

"Good morning, my two favorite people on the planet!" I heard Layla say. "How are we today?"

"Very well, thank you," said Frances. I heard sizzling

118

coming from the kitchen and knew that a batch of crispy bacon would accompany the pancakes.

Someone put their arms around my neck, and I looked up into the smiling brown eyes of the best (and admittedly only) girlfriend I'd ever had. "Good morning to you, too," I said to Layla. "How was your sleep?"

"Great!" Layla responded. "I had this really wonky dream where I was having tea—which is weird because I never have tea, unless it's chamomile—with Mark Twain, the White Rabbit, and Percy Jackson. Weird. But at the same time, cool. There was this all-women rock band playing in the background. It was great."

"Glad to hear it," I said. "No dreams, as usual. I had a pretty good night's sleep."

"What'd I say?" Layla said, grinning. "Kissing helps."

This made me crack up. "Yeah, I guess it does," I managed through my laughter. "Want some coffee? I can get you some."

"That would be great, thanks," said Layla as she plopped down on the couch.

I got up and got Layla some coffee. As I handed it to her and sat down beside her, my parents came in.

My parents were in a new movie that was supposed to be really, really good, and part of it was being filmed in Brazil, so they hadn't been around a lot. But when they *were* home, they were super awesome. Mom was tan and had a brand-new perm, and Dad had a serious farmer's tan and was still bald. Both were great parents. Dad had taught me how to read and write way before first grade, and Mom had taught me the rules of softball, which I had ended up playing all throughout junior high and high school. Both had cheerfully accepted that ghosts were real and among us, and they had remained perfectly sane in the process.

In fact, they'd loved that I'd gotten to see Cassidy often,

and while they declined the opportunity to go themselves—it was just too painful for them, which I understood—they encouraged me to communicate with her often and sent her messages all the time through me.

So, yeah. In short, they were great.

"Mom!" I shouted, jumping up and hugging my parents. "I missed you! You were gone for weeks!"

"I know," Mom sighed. "Brazil is wonderful, and the locals are simply lovely, but honestly, the heat really gets to me sometimes. And the mosquitoes are quite annoying." To prove her point, she scratched a nasty-looking mosquito bite on her elbow.

"Don't scratch at it, Mom," I said. "That'll only make it worse. If you really have to, do it with your knuckles, not with your nails." This ingenious little trick had saved me many a scab.

"I suppose you're right," Mom said, removing her hand from her elbow.

"How you doing, sweetie?" Dad asked. "Everything been okay while we've been gone?"

"Yeah," I said, then remembered Cassidy and my little problem with entering the Ghost Realm. "Well, actually, not really."

Dad's bearded face creased in concern. "*Not really?* What's wrong?"

"You guys should probably sit down for this," I said. I knew that they'd blow both of their tops, and I fiddled with my thumbs nervously. But I just said it: "The Ghost Realm is now closed."

As predicted, my parents *did* freak out. Dad got up and ran a full twenty laps around the perimeter of the family room, then sat down again and uttered some very bad words. Mom was so upset she ruined her perm and grabbed the nearest pillow and mashed her face into it.

I watched all of this guiltily. Why I felt guilty, I couldn't say. I knew it wasn't my fault, but tell that to my emotions. Fortunately, Layla came to my rescue, and using her superpower, she managed to calm everyone down enough for me to fully explain what was going on.

I cleared my throat nervously and looked down at my hands, which were sweaty and twitching anxiously. I had some sort of rousing speech planned in my mind, but I'd never been good at talking while a large number of people stared bug-eyed at me. "Um. Well. Hi, everybody. How are we all doing? Great, glad to hear that . . . "

My parents and even Layla stared at me with funny expressions on their faces.

"Just get on with it, Eda," said Dad.

"Right, right, sorry. Well, um, as you know, the Ghost Realm is no longer free to access," I said. I looked down at the imaginary index cards in my sweaty hands. "Cassidy recently sent an email featuring the lyrics of a song from my favorite movie, explaining that the Ghost Realm has been relocated to an impossible-to-find place due to the unfortunate disappearances of several sections of it. No explanation for the disappearances has been enclosed, so I know very little. Most likely, we won't be able to contact her again." I swallowed. "I think . . . I think that email was . . . was goodb—" I couldn't choke the word out. It refused to leave my mouth, and I felt a lump form in my throat. I wiped my hands on my pants, but that did nothing to dry them.

Layla's hand closed around mine, squeezing it tightly. "Eda," she said. "We know."

I sniffled and wiped at my eyes with my free hand. "I just . . . I just want to see her again. Why is that so hard?"

Layla said nothing, just hugged me tight. Mom and Dad sat beside me and awkwardly offered their condolences while also, it seemed, managing their own sadness about a more complete disconnection from Cassidy.

All this attention was suddenly stifling. I pushed away from Layla and my parents and went upstairs to my room. I slammed the door shut behind me, angry all of a sudden. I needed to throw something.

I seized my favorite stuffed animal—a cute little elephant affectionately named Ellie—and hurled her at the wall. I repeated this again and again and again until all the anger drained out of me. I felt like a hurricane of different feelings, and it was all so overwhelming.

I walked over and picked Ellie up from where she'd fallen and ran my hand over her gray plush. Then I apologized to her and collapsed on my bed. I curled up, clutching Ellie to my chest, and cried and cried and cried.

Hours seemed to pass as I lay there, and it probably was hours. Multiple times, people knocked on my door, but I just rolled over and screamed at them to go away.

Not the best family reunion.

I woke up from the light doze I'd taken. It was day out, and my clock said it was noon. Ellie was soaked with tears, and there was a small rip in her ear from when she'd caught on something sharp when I had thrown her. I fingered the rip. "Sorry, Ellie," I mumbled, my eyes stinging from tears. "I wish I hadn't thrown you. I'll fix you up soon, I promise."

Yawning, I stumbled out of bed and found a needle and thread of the same shade as Ellie's plush. I stitched her ear back together, and I lay back down again. I looked into Ellie's black glass eyes, and even though I knew she wasn't alive and that she couldn't hear me, I talked to her. "I'm mad, Ellie," I said. "Cassidy won't see me anymore. And she didn't even tell me what was going on until now. And she wants me to trust her, but how can I trust her right now?" I wiped at my eyes and continued. "I really miss her, though. I want to hear her voice again. I want to jump off of buildings in Heaven with her again. I'm also really, really, really sad. My whole life, she's been there for me. And now she's gone."

I squeezed Ellie a final time and closed my eyes, drifting off to sleep again.

Later in the day, there was a knock at the door. This wasn't so unusual—just about every half-hour, my parents had come to check on me, but I knew immediately that it was someone other than my mother or father. Dad had a firm, decisive knock, like the way a lawyer would knock; Mom had a softer, more rapid way of knocking. But Layla had a loud, banging knock: BANG, BANG, BANG BAM. "Let me in!"

I climbed out of bed and opened the door about an inch. "Yeah?"

"Hey, Eda. Can I come in?" Layla asked.

I opened the door wider. "Sure, whatever."

Layla stepped into my room. I had always been a bit of a neat freak, so everything was very tidy and orderly (I couldn't stand crooked picture frames). The only things that were untidy were the stuffed animals I'd thrown and hadn't bothered to pick up yet.

Layla gave me a plate full of pancakes. "Leftovers. From earlier," she said. "We saved 'em for you."

"Thanks, I guess," I said. I picked up the fork beside the plate and took a bite.

Layla sat on the edge of my bed. "So, how're you feeling?" she asked.

"Not great." I viciously stabbed another chunk of pancake and shoved it in my mouth.

"I can see that. You've apparently locked your parents out

all day," Layla said. "I wasn't there for most of it, because I had to babysit Andrew, but when I came back, your parents were literally begging me to go check on you because you wouldn't let them in. I didn't want to—I told them it was better if we let you process your feelings in your own way—but then," Layla offered me an apologetic smile, "they threw in two jumbo bars of dark chocolate."

"Mm-hmm," I said as I reached for one.

"No problem." Layla reached into her coat pocket and brought out something. "I also snatched a whole bag of your favorite treat on my way up for you." She put the bag in my hand. "A *whole bag*. I felt like a spy when I was doing that."

I took the bag and read the label. "Stroopwafels?" I said. I quickly took the twist tie off and happily stuck one of the crunchy, chewy mini-waffles in my mouth.

"Feeling better now?" Layla asked, watching me chew.

"Yup," I spoke around the food in my mouth. "Stroopwafels solve everything."

Layla laughed. "Okay, well, I gotta go. Your parents are probably itching to know what happened. Come down when you're ready, okay? And if you're not ready . . . well, then, don't come down."

I grinned. "Okay. Bye."

"Bye," Layla said as she got up and shut the door behind her.

I finished eating and stashed the remaining stroopwafels in a dresser drawer, then crawled back into bed. I hugged Ellie and stared at the ceiling, which was painted a very boring light gray. "Cassidy," I muttered, "where are you?"

About an hour later, I finally got up and dragged myself out of bed because laying there doing nothing was so mind-numbingly boring. Instead of going downstairs, where Layla and my parents were likely waiting, I crossed the hall to Cassidy's old room.

Pac-Man wasn't there (he was on a date with Seamus), but Alfie was. This time he was awake, playing poker against his old friend Sally, who was visiting today. I entered the room just as Sally was dealing the cards, passing them around in seemingly empty space. Sally was sharing Alfie's computer screen, so I could clearly see her dark, white-streaked hair styled in a chignon, her plain white blouse and baby-blue skirt, and her dimpled face creased with smile wrinkles.

"Hey, guys," I said from the doorway. "Am I bothering you?"

Both shook their heads. "No, not at all," said Alfie. He motioned to a chair. "Please sit. Do you want me to deal you in?"

"Nah, thanks. I don't play poker." I eased myself onto the wicker rocking chair in front of the computer screen. "I just want to talk to you about something."

"Both of us, or just Alfie?" Sally asked.

"Just Alfie," I said. "Sorry to interrupt your game."

"Oh, that's fine," said Alfie. "We only just started. Sally, would you mind leaving for a few minutes?"

"Nope. I'll be in the Coleman house next door if you need me." Sally's face disappeared from the screen.

Alfie laced his fingers. "What do you want to talk about, child?"

"Well, you know about how Cassidy hasn't been talking to me?" I began.

Alfie nodded, his head of curls flying as well.

"I got a message from her earlier."

"But, Eda, that's *great!*" Alfie exclaimed.

"Yeah, not really," I said. Since I had long since memorized the entire email, I quoted it for him. After I was done, Alfie sat there for a while, deep in thought (I thought he looked quite philosophical, actually).

"Eda," Alfie said at last, "this situation has turned out to be much graver than I thought."

"Do you know what her email means?" I asked eagerly.

Alfie shook his head. "No, child, I'm afraid not."

My spirits fell immediately. "Oh."

"But," Alfie added, "I'll do some research on the Internet. The Internet is like the smorgasbord of the digital world; there's bound to be something in there."

I brightened. "Really? You'd do that for me?"

"Of course I would, child!" Alfie thundered. "Why wouldn't I?"

"Good point," I said.

"Oh, yoo-hoo!" Sally said, appearing on the computer screen. "Time's up!"

I smiled at them. "Yeah, I should probably go now, anyway. I'll let you get back to your game."

"Bye, Eda," said Sally before the two ghosts picked up their cards again.

I quietly slipped out of the room and went downstairs. No one was there. There was a note on the dining table:

Eda—

Me and Dad going out to dinner. Layla has gone home, but if you need her, just call her. Frances has gone on break for a couple days, so make sure to make dinner for yourself.

My phone number is taped onto the back of your computer so you don't forget it.

Love you, sweetheart

—*Mom*

I sighed and looked at the clock. 4:30. I'd been stuck in my room all day.

I made myself an early dinner of mac 'n' cheese and ate on the couch. I texted Layla and some pen pals from Belgium for a while before saying goodbye. I washed my dishes and then finally got dressed in a pair of sweatpants and a Boston Red Sox shirt that Dad had gotten for me for Christmas a year ago just because he liked the team (seriously).

I went outside for a while because I had been crammed inside my house for a long time. I needed some fresh air.

It was getting dark, so I took a flashlight that doubled as a portable speaker and slipped it into my pocket. I also took my phone (because I wasn't stupid), put on a pair of tall insulated boots, and walked outside.

It was December, and therefore, it was very cold. But I was resistant to temperatures, so I wasn't bothered much. The walkway to my house was conveniently cleared of snow, and I had no trouble getting across.

I chose a random course—modern GPS made it impossible to get lost—and walked aimlessly for a while. I admired the mountains that rose up before me and the beautiful scenery.

And somehow, while I was walking around like this, I ended up on Layla's porch.

Layla lived by herself in a house painted a delicate pale pink. She had a porch swing because she loved them, and whenever holidays like Christmas and Halloween came around, she would always decorate her house and yard elaborately. Last year, she had decorated her yard with an army of elves surrounding a female Santa Claus and Mrs. Claus. This time, she had wrapped her house from head to toe in Christmas lights, even decorating the trees in her yard.

Closing my eyes so as not to be blinded by the blinking, flashing, and occasionally beeping lights that completely enwrapped Layla's house, I climbed the stairs to her porch and knocked on the door.

When she opened it, she immediately pulled me into a tight hug and led me to her couch, over which she had thrown a soft blanket covered in kittens wearing Santa hats. It was both the most wonderful and the tackiest thing I'd ever seen. When we sat down, my butt sank about an inch, the couch was so soft.

"So," said Layla as we sat down, "do you like this year's decorations or what?"

"I love them," I said truthfully. "They are really quite something."

"Yeah, they are," Layla said. Then she leaned in and whispered, "Don't tell anybody, but I reused my decorations from four years ago."

"They're still great," I said.

Layla leaned back and lounged casually on the couch. "So, Eda, you finally got up. I congratulate you."

"I was upset," I said.

"That much was clear," said Layla. "Why'd you come to my house, of all places?"

I shrugged. "Honestly, I don't know. I was just walking around randomly, and somehow, I ended up here."

"Maybe it was true love that brought you here," Layla teased.

I swatted at her arm. "No, it was not. It was just a coincidence."

"Or was it?" Layla said mysteriously.

"Did you have too much eggnog?" I asked.

"Nah, I didn't have any eggnog yet," said Layla. "I was waiting to share it with you."

"Oh."

Outside, a light snow started to fall, illuminated by the sun sinking into the horizon.

I pointed at it. "That's really pretty," I said.

Layla looked, too. "Yeah, it is."

We sat staring for a while, but then the sun finally slipped out of sight, and darkness fell.

"So," said Layla finally, "whaddya want to do?"

"I dunno," I said. "Maybe investigate Cassidy's email."

"I *knew* you'd bring that topic up!" Layla said triumphantly. She scooted closer to me. "Well, I don't know about you, but I think better on a full stomach. Let's have dinner first, then decode it."

"Okay," I agreed. "Worth a shot." I had eaten earlier, but I was still hungry, and Layla was a really good cook (not as good as Frances, though).

Layla hopped off of the couch and began bustling around in the kitchen while I played games on my phone. After a while, the whole house was filled with the smell of food, and my stomach rumbled, reminding me of my hunger.

"Dinner time!" Layla sang as she carried plates over to the table. "No eating on the couch because it is a nice couch, and I don't want it to get ruined."

I got up and joined my girlfriend at the table. She passed me a plate, and I looked at the food on it: French toast drowned in syrup. Possibly her favorite thing to make because it involved a lot of sugar.

"Isn't French toast a breakfast food?" I asked.

Layla looked offended. "Of course not! It can be served at every single meal and still taste good."

"Right, right," I said. "Sorry I asked."

After we ate, I helped Layla clear the table and put the dirty dishes in the dishwasher, and then we sat back down on the couch.

I picked up my phone. "Let's start with what we know. We know Cassidy is in some weird place we can't find, and guests aren't permitted in their new Ghost Realm."

"There is not a lot we do know," said Layla.

"Correct. Now, let's move on to what we *don't* know," I said.

"Which is a whole lot more," said Layla.

"Also correct." I thought back to Cassidy's note. "Is it possible to be between the north and the south and the east and the west?" I asked.

"Well . . . " Layla said slowly. "Maybe. Maybe the place Cassidy is talking about isn't related to the song; maybe it's just a coincidence. Maybe the new Ghost Realm is somewhere right on the equator. And maybe it's on an island."

"Like the Bahamas or something?"

Layla nodded. "Yeah, like the Bahamas."

"Hmm," I said. "What about the Bermuda Triangle?"

"You mean the spot where ships and airplanes always seem to go missing?" Layla said.

"Yeah, that's a place where people don't really go very often," I said. "It's the perfect place for a new Ghost Realm."

Layla thought this over. "You're right," she said at last. "It *is* the perfect place for a new Ghost Realm."

"Layla, how do you like the idea of a vacation?" I asked.

"I like it very much," said Layla. "My nephew is cute and all, and I do get thirty dollars every time I babysit him, but it can become a bit much after a while."

"Excellent," I said, feeling like an evil genius when I used the word. I pulled out my phone. "I'm booking a trip for three to Florida. We can go into the Bermuda Triangle via boat or plane from there."

"Who's the third person?" Layla inquired.

"Uncle Pac-Man," I answered, busying myself with my phone. "He'll want to see Cassidy, probably."

Layla held out her fist, and I bumped it, making a funny explosion noise. "Eda Weldon, I do believe we're one step closer to finding your sister."

CHAPTER
ELEVEN

When I told Pac-Man the news later that evening, he shouted "HALLELUJAH!," jumped up and down excitedly, asked, "Should I bring my red hippo-patterned swim trunks or my green striped swim trunks?" (Alfie responded that he should definitely bring the green striped swim trunks), and let loose a long string of very happy-sounding words in Norwegian. I had picked up enough Norwegian from him over the years to recognize some of what he was saying: "Oh, glorious, glorious day!" and "What a stupendous, beautiful, wonderful day!" (even though it was nighttime).

Finally, Pac-Man got ahold of himself and sat down. "So what do we do now?"

"Well, first, we should start packing," I told him. "Remember, it's Florida, so no need for warm layers. We'll leave tomorrow afternoon and return three days later."

"Woo-hoo!" Pac-Man scampered off upstairs, and I heard him throwing things around.

"You were right," said Layla after Pac-Man disappeared. "He does appear to be very happy."

"Yup." I grinned, proud of myself. "He doesn't get to visit Cass very often, so this is a special treat for him."

"Well, I suppose I should start packing too," said Layla. "I should go home now and start. No time like the present, right?"

"Right," I smiled. "See you tomorrow, Layla."

"See ya." We kissed, and Layla went out the door. I heard her fifty-year-old car (it used to belong to her father) roar to life, and she backed out of the driveway and sped away into the night.

I went up to my room and started raiding my closet.

I dug out my old gray suitcase and laid it open on the floor. I packed enough clothing for a week, even though we would only be staying for a few days, brushed my teeth, and then put my toothbrush, toothpaste, and floss inside a little baggie. I packed Ellie the elephant for extra emotional support.

Then I went through everything I had packed to make sure it was enough, double-checking that I hadn't forgotten my underwear (which had actually happened once), triple-checking that Ellie was secure and comfy, and quadruple-checking that I hadn't forgotten to pack my favorite Paisley shirt.

Finally, I surveyed the contents of my suitcase and officially declared that my packing was complete.

I went into Pac-Man's room—a.k.a. the Man Cave, because my uncle claimed that he liked the sound of it—to check on his progress. Unsurprisingly, clothing, ancient Spider-Man comics, and (yuck) random underwear were strewn across the floor.

Uncle Pac-Man was standing in front of a full-length mirror in his hippo bathing suit.

"I thought Alfie suggested the green."

"He did," Uncle Paco said, "but what does a millennia-old Roman know about modern fashion?" He turned toward me. "I like these."

I sighed. He looked ridiculous, but what did I care, especially when I had more serious things to worry about? "So any idea how we get sucked into the Bermuda Triangle?"

Pac-Man sat down and folded his legs, squeezing several hippos tight in the process. "I was just thinking about that. I'm guessing the best thing to do is just fly through it."

"Okay," I said, "but don't planes fly through it all the time? How are we going to be sure we're the ones who get, er, disappeared?" I plopped down next to Paco, my earlier enthusiasm waning slightly.

"Kiddo, we can't control everything. This is a good plan, and we may just have to have a little faith." He rubbed my back. "I expect that Cassidy will grab us if we get close enough."

"Like King Kong?" I asked as I laughed. Mom had insisted I watch that old movie when I was a kid, and the special effects were terrible. But I did like the idea of my big sister as a giant gorilla.

"Something like that," Pac-Man said. "Now, did you pack a swimsuit?"

"Of course," I said. "But mine is a simple blue bikini, no hippos."

"What a shame," Pac-Man said.

Our flight to Daytona left the next morning, on December 24, and after parking Layla's massive old car in the long-term garage, we checked in, went through security—Pac-Man got chosen for a random security search, probably because he had insisted on wearing the hippo suit for the flight—and finally made it onto the plane. I'd splurged and had gotten us first-class tickets. Well, I hadn't actually splurged. I'd just used a few of the airline miles Dad had been saving for the mysterious "later" he always mentioned when Mom suggested they take a vacation. He had 8,543,221 miles even after our tickets, so I didn't feel bad at all.

After my uncle finished explaining that he was not a maniac with a terrible sense of fashion to the flight attendant greeting us, we hustled onboard and slid into our seats.

Planes these days were not too different from the old early twenty-first-century ones when it came to looks, but scientists had figured out how to make them more carbon-efficient, which was great because global warming wasn't being very friendly to Earth. Also, some were robot-piloted, and I was pretty sure that the plane we had just boarded was fireproof.

Pac-Man sat closest to the tiny oval-shaped window (darn!), and I was squeezed in between him, Layla, and some old lady. He had gotten ahold of the TV remote and was now messing around with the TV channels, and eventually, I made him put the thing back in its little container. Uncle Pac-Man was a great guy, but sometimes he acted like a sixth grader.

"How long is the flight gonna last?" Pac-Man asked after opening a comic book, reading half a page, and then closing it again.

I sighed. "A few hours." I had been told that when I was born, it took several hours to get from my small town in Virginia to Orlando, Florida. Daytona was about fifty-one miles from Orlando on the Atlantic coast, so it was probably at least an hour away. But now, thanks to improved methods of transportation, getting to Daytona would likely take only three hours at the most.

"Oh," said Pac-Man. "You know, back in my day—"

I cut him off. "Yeah, I know. You've told me that about a million times."

Pac-Man opened his comic book again and started reading.

I checked the weather app on my phone. No snow—it never snowed in Florida—but it would be colder than usual and cloudy. I'd take what I could get.

Layla nudged me. "Hey. What's going on in that beautiful, attractive green head of yours?"

"Guess," I said.

'You're thinking about how wonderful I am?"

I laughed. "Hah, no. I'm thinking about how there's no snow in Florida."

"Of course there's no snow," said Layla. "It's *Florida*, Eda."

"I know it's Florida," I said.

"Right. Just checking. Anyway, I wanted to bring my surf-board, but, y'know, it's huge, and there's not enough room in my suitcase. Also, I don't think airports let people walk around with gigantic neon-colored boards," said Layla. "But I brought two pairs of oxygen Ts because I knew you'd probably forget yours."

I grinned. Layla knew me well.

Oxygen Ts were what they sounded like: T-shaped pieces of hard plastic that filtered oxygen from the water so you could breathe while beneath the surface. If you've watched the old Star Wars movie with Qui-Gon and the young Obi-Wan Kenobi, the oxygen Ts basically looked like those breathy thin-gies that they used while in the giant lake. I constantly forgot mine, so I had to get my oxygen the old-fashioned way.

Layla slung her arm around my back. "So, what's the plan for finding the Ghost Realm?" she asked.

"Well," I answered, "Uncle Pac-Man thinks we should just take a plane and go plunging into the Bermuda Triangle, but I think we should find somebody with a motorboat big enough for several people and take it a little slower. Going fast can be great, but sometimes you can miss a bunch of important things." I glanced at Pac-Man; he was still engrossed in his reading, unaware that anything important was going on.

"I think that's a good idea, too," said Layla. "Sometimes I get really impatient during a test, so I just go really fast. But then I find that I did really poorly because I rushed."

I nodded. "Same here. I think we've all had that experience."

A flight attendant pushed her trolley through the aisle and stopped at our row of seats. "Y'all want anything? I have water, Coke, Sprite, Mountain Dew, Red Bull, root beer, lemonade, fruit juice, and three different assortments of tea for drinks. For snacks, I have mini pretzels, Doritos, Cheetos, and containers of fruit."

I requested some Doritos and a Coke; Layla ordered a Mountain Dew. "We can share the Doritos; it's a romantic thing to do," she told me. Pac-Man looked up from his Spider-Man comics long enough to order Cheetos and a Coke, and the lady to Layla's right smiled cheerfully and asked for some water.

Then we all settled in with our food and drinks. I slurped at my Coke while Layla ate most of my Doritos, Pac-Man shoved Cheetos into his mouth, staining the pages of his precious book with orange powder, and the lady sipped at her water with her pinky finger up daintily.

"Are you guys going to Daytona too?" asked the lady after she set her drink down. She looked sort of like the long-deceased Queen Elizabeth the Second—she had short, curly white-gray hair on which a baby-blue hat with a ribbon on it sat, wore an equally blue dress, and had a squat frame with deep wrinkles on her face. It took me a minute to absorb this. To some less kind people, she would look simply absurd due to her fashion choices. Dresses had been practically eliminated years ago in America—you occasionally saw them at weddings, but many brides had started dressing like the grooms.

I took another drink of Coke and then replied, "Yeah, we're going to Daytona."

"Really!" the woman said excitedly. "Well, I'm going there to meet my new grandson. His name is Sydney, and he is just the cutest thing you ever saw."

I could practically hear Layla thinking, *Bet he's not as cute as my nephew.*

"I'm sure he is," I said politely. "We're going to see family too. My sister, in fact."

"Oh, how lovely! I hope you have a simply wonderful family reunion," said the old woman.

I thought, *If I even get to see her again.* "Thanks," I said to her. "I hope you have a great time with your family."

"Thank you, young lady," said the woman. "You really are very kind."

I nodded, blushing a little, and reached back into the bag of Doritos, only to discover that Layla had finished them off. I gave her a look that said, *You owe me another bag of Doritos,* and she met my gaze with an innocent expression that asked, *Who, me?*

The rest of the flight passed surprisingly quickly, and I was a little startled when the flight attendant announced that we would be landing in ten minutes. I quickly downed the rest of my second Coke and felt the sugar coursing through my system.

The plane landed, and we clambered off, filing into the Daytona airport. I took a bathroom break and rejoined my girl-friend and uncle outside.

Layla hailed a taxi, and we struggled to heave our luggage into the trunk. Then we all went inside, with me wedged between my two companions.

The taxi was driven by a man with a mullet, a mustache, a red jacket, a twangy Southern accent when he spoke, and a random dolphin sticker plastered to his forehead, which was rare because most service vehicles nowadays were either driven by robots or were self-driving. "Hiya, folks! Welcome to Russell Taxicab Services and—oh, forget it. It's a stupid customary introduction that every passenger has to listen to. Why do we even do it? I dunno. Anyway, I'm Russell, and I'll be your taxi driver today. No, Russell Taxicab Services is not named after me; it's just some weird coincidence."

"Hey, Russell," Pac-Man said. "Can you take us to the Portman Hotel? I'm sorry, I don't know the address."

"Because you weren't listening when we reviewed this with you," Layla said.

"Now, calm down, folks," said Russell, twirling the pointy end of his mustache around his finger. "No need to have a full-blown conniption. This is supposed to be a safe and comfortable environment. Just read the words inscribed on the door."

I looked at the spot he was pointing at: ***Russell Taxicab Services: The Safest, Most Comfortable Place You Can Find When On the Move.***

Pac-Man and Layla bit back whatever unpleasant things they were going to say to each other and slumped back in their seats.

"So," Russell continued, "in response to your question, mister, yeah, I can."

"Good," said Pac-Man, relieved. "Now, how do I pay?"

Russell gave him a tablet with a pen. "You just sign here, and Russell Taxicab Services does the rest."

"Okay," said Pac-Man. He signed it, and Russell took it back.

Russell squared his shoulders and gripped the steering

wheel. "All righty, folks. We should arrive at Portman Hotel in, oh, say, five minutes."

"Excellent," I said.

"Now, I should warn y'all, this baby here"—Russell patted the dashboard in what seemed to be affection—"really likes to go fast. So, maybe find somethin' to hold on to and hold on to it hard. And when I say hard, I mean *real* hard."

"Why?" I asked. "It can't be that ba—*HOLY #$%!*" The car lurched forward, leaving the contents of my stomach behind. I swear that sparks literally flew from the bottoms of the tires, and the roar of the engine was so loud I could barely hear myself think. We shot past buildings and other cars, and I heard somebody screaming, only to discover that it was me. Russell drove like a man possessed, his mustache flying.

"FUN, RIGHT?!" Russell yelled, turning to look at us.

"*FUN?*" I shrieked.

"ARE YOU DEAF? YES, FUN!" Russell shouted.

"*WATCH OUT FOR THAT BUILDING!*" I pointed.

Russell spun back around, yelled, "WHOA, BABY!" and jerked the steering wheel to the left.

Then, after careening through a couple more blocks, our gas-pedal-happy driver slammed his foot on the brakes, literally screeching to a noisy halt.

We sat there for a moment, panting. I looked at the tire marks he'd made on the pavement in front of the hotel. Yup. Those were never coming off.

Fortunately, at this particular hotel, I didn't think anyone would notice, not with the massive spotlights spinning through the air and the neon entranceway. Heck, if people could even see the street, they'd be lucky.

Despite its classy name, The Portman Hotel looked like it was the garish brainchild of Las Vegas and Dubai but with more lights. Even the sidewalk lit up, which led Layla to do a relatively good impression of that old classic video, *Billie Jean* by Michael Jackson. It was a miraculous place, and I was going to love every one of the 707 minutes we would be here.

On the flight, I had found a fishing trawler that accepted "whale watching" passengers for a small fee. The boat left in just over twelve hours, so we'd only be here one night. I was a bit disappointed, but my retinas were quite content to have a shorter stay.

Our room was only slightly less, um, festive, with neon running under the rims of the two beds and around every straight edge in the place. Even the bathtub featured a thermal mood light that changed as you moved through your bathing routine. I couldn't decide if I thought that was cool or just weird.

Fortunately, at 10 p.m., the lights went off. Unfortunately, *all* the lights went off, including the regular ones that let us, you know, see. So we were in bed early. It wasn't a bad thing, except that I hadn't yet gotten up the nerve to tell Uncle Pac-Man that we were getting up at 5 a.m. so we could catch our boat.

Also fortunately, the hotel had a very effective and snooze-proof wake-up call system, so at 5 a.m., when the house music started and all the lights came on, Uncle Pac-Man was upright in a flash, pun intended.

For the sake of decency, we all got dressed quickly, and then, because my uncle was always a little slow to fully wake up, even if his body was moving, we were able to coax him downstairs and into a cab with the promise of fresh-baked bread when we got to our next leg of the journey.

He was, however, fully conscious by the time we reached the fishing wharf, and let's just say our promise of fresh bread did not make up for the fishy smell, the impending sea sickness, and the hours on a boat—in his eyes, at least.

I, however, was thrilled. "I love that smell," I said into Layla's ear as the boat began to go out to sea.

"Me, too," she said before giving me a quick kiss and then immediately throwing up overboard. Uncle Pac-Man didn't look so good either, and so for most of the six-hour ride toward Bermuda, they bent over the sides while I used the only pair of binoculars to watch for whales while dodging the fishing nets coming in and out of the boat.

Sadly, whales had become almost extinct across their species. Huge pleasure boats and military operations had damaged their communication, and many of them had been injured in huge fossil fuel spills over the past fifty years. So I didn't, in fact, see any on our trip.

Porpoises, however, had managed to survive and actually thrive. I chalked this up to their far superior intelligence and the fact that they kept humans in their sights most of the time. Many people thought their propensity to swim beside boats was play, and that may have been part of their motivation, but I was convinced they also did this as surveillance. Smart guys, those ones.

Since Layla and Uncle Pac-Man were otherwise occupied, I devoted a lot of my time to talking with a particular porpoise, whom I'd dubbed Lucian. I knew my name of choice was probably a bit insulting, since I guessed the animal's replies in clicks and squeaks were probably based in some kind of quantum math sequence that had been converted into language, but I needed something to call him.

"Lucian, tell me about the Bermuda Triangle," I said about two hours into our trip.

The porpoise, who had been keeping pace with us easily for the entire trip, clicked up at me something that I chose to interpret as, "That place is a pit."

"Not great, huh?" I replied. "Heard anything about some ghosts moving in?"

He clicked a response that I took to be, "Oh yes, definitely. Hope they clean the place up."

We continued in this vein for another few hours off and on, and by the time we actually reached Bermuda, a feat achieved by the super-powered boat engine that moved the vessel along quite quickly even while the fishers used magnetic boots to stay on deck at top speed, I had a sense that Lucian and I would be lifelong friends and that I would need to introduce him to Cassidy since it seemed he had a very good lay of the land—er —the sea in these parts.

As the boat slowed to a halt at the edge of the invisible area called the Bermuda Triangle, I asked the captain if we might trouble him to go a bit farther. He seemed rather intrepid, and since his favorite films were the Pirates of the Caribbean ones – "I fancy meself a wizened Johnny Depp, ya know," he said at one point – I thought my request was a simple one. Boy, was I wrong.

"No, missy. I don't go into them here parts. Too many a sailor lost to these waters," he said, scratching his somewhat stereotypical white beard. "If we were coming in along the hypotenuse, I might risk it for ye, but not here. Too dangerous."

I stared at him for a minute. "Are you telling me the Bermuda Triangle is an actual triangle?"

He furrowed his brow and nodded. "What else would it be? One right angle just over there and two acute forty-five-degree ones there and there." He pointed to three spots in the ocean that looked like more ocean to me.

"All righty, then," I said. "So we can take the dinghy from here as agreed?"

"Aye, missy." He gestured toward a very iffy-looking boat that I doubted was even watertight. "Best boat in these parts, if

I do say so myself. Held together with rubber from trees I felled myself."

I thought it best not to point out that taking down any trees was a felony these days. I didn't fancy a swim with the fishes if he got offended.

"Well, thank you very much. We'll see you in three days if we see you at all," I said as I cranked the dinghy down into the water and then helped first Layla and then Uncle Pac-Man down the rope ladder on the side.

"I'll be here, Missy. Hope you will be, too." With that, he gave me a salute, untied the rope for the dinghy, and went back to the cabin. We were on our own.

Fortunately, the dinghy was powered by a pretty serious outboard motor, and once I figured out I didn't have to dislocate my shoulder pulling a cord, like they always did in the old movies, and could just press a button to start her up, we were off.

Fortunately, the mysteries of seasickness meant that both Layla and Uncle Pac-Man were far less ill on this tiny boat than they had been on the large one, so we all took turns steering the boat.

We had no real destination in mind. We just wanted to tool around the triangle and see if, by chance, we might discover anything about the Ghost Realm. Lucian's comments had given me hope, which I realized, even then, was a little silly since I hadn't understood a word he had said. Still, it was all I had to go on, and I was at the point where I would cling to any hope that I had.

"See that over there?" Uncle Pac-Man said after we'd been wandering aimlessly on the ocean sea for about a half hour. He was pointing ahead of us.

I leaned forward to see more clearly and then said, "You mean that strange line where the water seems to get lighter?"

"Oh, I see that," Layla said. "Must be the edge of the triangle."

I gaped at her. "Did you know it was an actual triangle, too?"

"What else would it be?" she said.

I rolled my eyes. "Well, if that's the edge, we might as well sail to that line and then hang a left."

"Agreed," Uncle Pac-Man said and charged the boat forward toward the light.

Just then, I heard what sounded like the largest spaghetti slurp in the entire world coming from the sky above us. And then, just like that, we were zipped up into the air and into what I could only describe as a giant multicolored cylinder.

I might have been more descriptive if I hadn't been so very startled, but at the moment, all I could think was "alien angels," and then I passed out.

When I came to, Layla was leaning over me and patting my cheek. "Wake up, Eda. You have *got* to see this."

I blinked and reached up to rub at my eyes, only to accidentally miss and hit my nose instead (ouch). "Wha?" I mumbled, still half-asleep.

Layla rubbed at my eyes for me. "C'mon, Eda. Wake up, or you'll miss it."

"Miss what?" This got me awake because I didn't like missing stuff.

Layla pointed at something, and I sat up to see it.

Holy bleep.

Our little dinghy was suspended in midair, right in the center of the eye of a huge rainbow hurricane. Yes, that's what I said: a huge rainbow hurricane. The roar of the rotating column of water was nearly deafening, drowning out the gentle creaking of the wood and the sputtering of the ancient motor. Pac-Man was at the helm with his mouth open, and

Layla crouched next to me, equally amazed in her own not-really-amazed way.

But that wasn't what I was really staring at.

Souls. I was looking at souls.

Glowing white figures swirled around in the walls of the hurricane, sometimes bumping into each other and then apologizing. I couldn't see their faces; mostly, they were just white blurs or blobs, and I could hear chatter in hundreds of different languages over the roar of the hurricane. The souls were slowly floating upward into a blinding light at the top of the hurricane. And as I lay on the boat, I realized that we were climbing closer to the light as well.

"Layla," I said over the white noise turned up to max volume, "d'you think this is the entrance to the Ghost Realm?"

"I dunno, Eda," Layla said. "For all I know, this is a totally normal thing in the Bermuda Triangle. But you usually don't see rainbow, ghost-filled hurricanes every day, now, do you?"

"Probably not," I said.

"Right," Layla said.

Uncle Pac-Man ran to where I sat, his purple Crocs squeaking against the wet wood. "Eda! You're awake!"

"Duh," said Layla.

Pac-Man ignored her. "Didja see the ghosts?"

"Yup," I said.

"I *told* you guys my hippo swim trunks would bring us good luck!" Pac-Man pointed at his shorts.

"Did you?" asked Layla. "'Cause I don't seem to remember that."

I slowly got up. My whole body felt weak, but that was to be expected, as I had just passed out. I walked to the helm of the dinghy to get a closer inspection of the ghosts. Since I was closer, I caught some glimpses of features: a crooked nose, a happy smile, a tuft of puffy hair. I assumed that these were the recent dead.

Pac-Man and Layla had finished their latest argument and joined me in ghost watching. This was almost better than seeing a whale, but since whales were rarer, and these ghosts were certainly not running out, I liked whale watching better.

After boarding the dinghy, Layla had donned her bikini so as not to get her clothing wet. Her oxygen T was stuck in a little strap on her bikini bottom, its red lights glowing cheerfully. I had put on my bikini too, but I had buttoned my colorful red palm-tree-patterned paisley shirt over it. Pac-Man had worn his hippo swim trunks the whole time, so I'd constantly gotten glimpses of smiling cartoon hippopotamuses. Now, I thought that we looked like a strange group: a bare-chested dude with hippo swim trunks, a thin green-haired woman with a slightly oversized paisley shirt floating around her like a cape, and a short woman with a huge tattoo of a Chinese dragon on her back. All of us were leaning against the railing of a small boat staring out at phantoms in a rainbow hurricane.

Within a few moments, we were less than eight inches away from the white light, and I reached out my long skinny arm. My hand plunged straight into the stuff, and the light felt heavy and warm. I pulled my arm back out and examined it. The light had condensed on my skin, leaving a bit of shimmery liquid on it.

"Wow," I breathed, touching the small puddle on the palm of my hand. "Amazing."

Pac-Man reached out and poked at my hand. "Feels kind of like cotton candy."

"It does," Layla agreed, touching the light.

Now the top of Pac-Man's head brushed against the stuff, and I laughed. The light pooled on his head, turning his bristly hairs white.

And then, with a final slurping noise, we were sucked all the way into the light.

"Hello and welcome to the Ghost Realm—hey, you're not dead!" said a familiar voice.

I opened my eyes and found myself standing at the front of a line of ghosts. I was in a lobby much like the one in the original Ghost Realm, except everything except for the ghosts themselves was colorful. I stood in front of a desk, and behind that desk was Greg.

"Greg?" I said. "Boy, am I glad to see you!"

"How on Earth did you find us?" Greg frowned.

"A little bit of luck and a little bit of ingenuity," I said. "Can you take me to Cassidy, please? It's urgent."

"How urgent is 'urgent'?" Greg asked.

"Like, so urgent that I can't wait another five minutes," I said.

Greg sighed and ran his fingers through his perfectly combed and gelled hair. "Fine. I can't take you myself, you understand; I've got ghosts to register, but my friend Art can."

"I know Art," I said.

"Good. They'll come pick you up in a few minutes. Next!"

I found a bench nearby, and Layla, Pac-Man, and I all sat down. I felt extremely out of place in a fancy lobby while dressed in nothing but a bikini and a paisley shirt, and I had no doubt that my two accomplices felt the same way.

After a few stressful minutes, Art arrived, looking entirely the same as the last time I'd seen them with a gray fauxhawk, round glasses, soft gray eyes, a face that looked like it had been carved from marble, and an expression like they had just swallowed something unpleasant. "Oh. It's you again," they said.

"Yep," I said with more cheerfulness than necessary because I was feeling a little mischievous and wanted to annoy Art. As their expression had morphed from unpleasant to "I just sucked on a lemon," I felt I had achieved my purpose. "Take me to my sister."

Art rolled their eyes. "How do you ask nicely?"

Layla stomped over. "We are not children who need to be taught our manners." Then she snapped her fingers in Art's face. "Come on. You heard her."

Normally, I found snapping to get someone's attention or help very rude, but today, I liked it. I kissed Layla's cheek and smiled as Art turned without another word and began leading us down a hallway.

The hallway led into another hallway, then another, and eventually, I figured out that the whole Ghost Realm was made up of one gigantic building. There were small numbers on each door that we passed: 1200, 1201, 1202. The doors had small windows in them with shades; some were pulled up, and ghosts glanced at us through the windows.

After walking through at least fifty different hallways, Art finally stopped in front of a door with the number 5235 on it. They knocked three times, stepped back, and waited.

"Hold up, I'm coming!" shouted a muffled voice from inside. My heart started training for a 5K race, and I fidgeted with the watch around my wrist.

There was a tiny *click* from the other end of the door, and it swung open, revealing my sister.

"*Cassidy!*" I said. My voice squeaked a bit when I said this, as I had been trying hard to contain my excitement.

Cassidy stared at me, bewildered. "*Eda?* What are you doing here?"

"What do you *think* I'm doing here?" I yelled, suddenly angry. "You disappeared without warning! You refused to communicate with me! You blocked me from entering the Ghost Realm! What the *hell*, Cassidy! I was *so freaking worried!*"

"Eda," said Cassidy quietly. "Look, I'm really, really

sorry—"

"Sorry?" I screamed, seizing her shoulders. I felt like throttling her; I was so mad. "Sorry?! How can you expect me to be all calm and collected like you are now when you literally just shut me out?"

"EDA!" Cassidy said. She didn't exactly shout, but she wasn't quiet either. She said it loudly and firmly, and the force behind the word shut me up. I stood there, panting, my face streaked with angry tears. I wiped my eyes with my sleeve and glared at her. "Eda. I am truly, absolutely, and completely sorry. I was trying to do what was best for the Ghost Realm and its inhabitants."

"*Do what's best for the Ghost Realm and its inhabitants?*" I repeated. "But what about me? Why did you block me out? And not only me but Uncle Pac-Man and Mom and Dad too. Why'd you do it?"

Cassidy heaved a big sigh, running a hand through her green hair, which was tied away from her face in a messy, imperfect bun. "Come on in, and I'll explain everything." She smiled at me apologetically but also with a hint of sadness. "I've got plenty of stroopwafels."

My sister held the door open wider, and Layla, Pac-Man, and I stepped inside. Art had long since disappeared to God-knew-where, probably going off to party with their fellow cynical friends.

Cassidy's apartment was not the same as her cozy little bungalow back in Heaven. It had four visible rooms and a bathroom, plus a tiny kitchen nestled in the corner of the dining room. In the family room, the room we had just entered, there was a small cluster of armchairs surrounding a coffee table. A TV was attached to the wall. Only a few pictures hung on the walls, and her Snoopy picture, which I had grown so fond of, was gone.

Cassidy motioned to the armchairs. "Have a seat."

I slid into one and looked up when I had gotten myself comfortable enough, and I realized that there was somebody sitting in the chair across from mine. He was dressed in a somber black suit with unruly gray hair, a serious expression, two small horns poking out from his forehead, a long, slender tail lying across his lap, and a red pitchfork leaning against one of the armrests.

After giving Pac-Man a huge hug, Cassidy plopped down onto the seat next to me and pointed at the man across from me. "That, Eda, is Harry Houdini, Vice Devil and expert plumber for the inhabitants of Hell." She then introduced the rest of us to her friend. "Mister Houdini is the one responsible for everything that has happened.'

Harry Houdini gave an awkward wave. "Hey there. Uh, I just want to say sorry for, you know, the events that have, uh, occurred."

"What happened?" I asked.

"Well," said Houdini reluctantly. "You see, I was—oh, Cassidy, why can't *you* tell her?"

"Because it's *your* fault, and *you* were the person who did it," Cassidy said sternly.

I glanced at the two of them. "Did what?"

"Just listen to him," said Cassidy.

Houdini sighed. "All right, fine." He met my eyes. "Ever since computers were invented, I have been fascinated by them. I'm from the mid-twentieth century, after all, so that should make sense. So several weeks ago, I was fooling around with my computer during a meeting with the Devil, a little-known guy named Theodore Humphrey (before he died, he was one of the folks who sold George Washington the horse that he later rode into battle), and I, uh, accidentally erased a good-sized portion of Sunshine Plantation along with forty-one of its residents (that includes Benjamin Franklin—sorry, Ben). And then the computer somehow got a virus and started randomly annihilating several more places. I couldn't stop it. Sorry."

"And then, because the Ghost Realm was disappearing, Cassidy had to find everybody a new home quickly so that they wouldn't disappear with the Realm?" I said, catching on.

Cassidy nodded. "We didn't know what would happen if guests kept coming into the Ghost Realm during that time, so we had to bar them from entering. Even you, Eda. And I was so busy arranging stuff that I forgot to contact you. And when I did remember, I decided not to. I didn't know what it could do to the Ghost Realm. I thought it might be possible the presence of living people could throw off the precarious balance we were barely maintaining and erase us all."

"Then, to repent for my damages, I helped Cassidy out a bit," Houdini chimed in.

"He did," said Cassidy. "We quickly transferred the rest of the ghosts over here before the old Ghost Realm completely winked out of existence, and we've been here ever since." She looked at Houdini. "We were in such a hurry that we put everybody in the same place, so we currently don't have a Heaven or a Hell. We're working on fixing that. There are reports that Vlad the Impaler is giving his neighbors a tough time. But Houdini has been trying to help, and I really do appreciate that."

"Carrie Nation was particularly hard to handle," said Houdini. "She was threatening the couple next door when she found a half-empty glass of wine in the husband's hand. And when I stepped in to stop her, she threatened me, too. And she had a hatchet in her hand. I thought we had taken all forms of weapons away from her, but apparently not."

"Naturally," said Cassidy, "we moved her to a room next to a bunch of non-drinkers."

"Yes, I found that that helped tremendously. I do try to avoid her whenever I can, though," Houdini added.

I felt satisfied now that I had received some decent answers. I wasn't angry anymore, only slightly annoyed at the both of them. I shifted my position on the chair. "Can you tell me about your job, Houdini?"

"Well, for starters, it's not like you think it is," Houdini began. "Sure, I have horns, but every single Devil and Vice Devil has had horn implants. It's kind of a, how should I say this, symbolic thing. Devils and Vice Devils help keep all the naughty folks in check. They're like the presidents of Hell, actually. They are also part of the Council of the Gods, which convenes every two months and is held in a very, very, very big room, as there are a *lot* of gods. I have become close friends with a lovely young god named Hermes, in fact."

This made sense. Houdini was very similar to Hermes.

So Houdini told me all about life as a VID (Very Important Devil). He got free Dutch chocolate, free tickets to every single Ghostbusters football game (the Ghostbusters were a very popular team in Hell), and free access to Heaven and the Ghost Realm. He hadn't been put in Hell because he was a bad person; in fact, he'd started out in the Ghost Realm. But apparently, some sort of god saw potential in him and got him elected as Vice Devil. This was now his third time in office.

I had a lovely conversation with Houdini. Layla joined in too, and we all enjoyed our stroopwafels. Pac-Man caught up with Cassidy, but by the time Cassidy said we should go, I didn't want to leave. Why should I leave, anyway? Humans were well on their way to effectively and efficiently destroying the planet. I wanted to stay with my sister, too. But then I thought about my parents and all of the other people I'd come to love and who'd come to love me back. I couldn't stay, not yet, anyway.

So, a bit reluctantly, I got up to leave. As Layla, Pac-Man, and I stood in the doorway, Cassidy suddenly flung her arms around me. "See ya in a few years, sis," she mumbled into my shoulder.

I hugged her back. "See ya, Cass." Five years was going to be a long time, but at least I knew I could come back now.

"I love you," she muttered, her voice muffled from shoving her face into my shoulder. I felt weird, hugging someone while in nothing but a bathing suit in an environment where decent clothing was generally required, but I pushed this thought out of my mind and focused on her.

"Love you too." I squeezed her a final time, and we stepped back, our eyes wet.

"Paco," Cassidy said to my uncle. "It's . . . really good to see you again in person."

Pac-Man sniffled, wiping at his nose. "Yeah, it is."

"Remember when we were kids, and you snarfed down like ten cups of that gummy bear ice cream?" Cassidy asked him.

Pac-Man smiled. "Yeah. I got a major brain freeze, but I didn't tell you."

"And I had to clean up after you. It was really irritating, but at least you didn't spill," Cassidy told him.

Pac-Man laughed. "Love you, Cass."

"Love you too. Now, come on and give me a hug, you big Neanderthal," said Cassidy, spreading her arms open wide. Pac-Man went in for the hug, wrapping his long arms around her. He dwarfed her, and I imagined that it was very uncomfortable for both of them.

"Bye," I said to Cassidy.

"Bye, guys." Cassidy waved. My vision grew fuzzy, and soon everything turned black.

CHAPTER

TWELVE

I awoke to the sound of rain. It fell in a vicious torrent, soaking my clothing and causing it to cling to my skin. I pried my eyes open and sheltered them with my hand as I looked around me, still slightly groggy. The rainbow hurricane was no longer there, but a full-blown thunderstorm was. Lightning crackled and leapt across the roiling mass of dark clouds that blocked out the sky and sun. Thunder boomed, and I jumped; it sounded like it was right next to my ear.

I squinted through the downpour. We were on our little dinghy, still suspended in midair. I glanced down below and let out a shriek; we were so high up sea birds were flying below us. I gripped the railing of the boat and took in some deep breaths to try to calm down, which wasn't easy because there was a threat of accidentally sucking water up my nose.

Layla and Pac-Man were sprawled out next to me, still unconscious. Both were snoring, loud enough to be heard over the thunder.

Then there was a snapping sound like a rubber band being stretched taut and then let go, and our dinghy fell.

We fell like lead weights. There was nothing to stop us or break our descent except the crashing waves below us, and I really didn't want to belly flop onto those waves. I scrambled to get a grip on something—anything—and that something turned out to be Layla.

I closed my eyes and grabbed Layla, hugging her like the world was coming to an end. We fell for what seemed like an eternity while I prayed over and over that I wouldn't die, the wind roaring in my ears, tears leaking from my eyes.

But then:

CRASH!

The dinghy smashed into the tumultuous surface of the water, instantly breaking into hundreds of pieces. The sheer force of it hitting the water sent me reeling backward, still clinging to Layla tightly. A huge wave that, on a nice day, would be like a surfer's paradise rose over us and buried us in water.

The pressure of the water shoved Layla and me into the water, forcing me to let go of her. We drifted away, and I struggled to get back to her. My lungs were aching for air, so I quickly grabbed her hand and propelled us to the surface. I was glad that I had been a lifeguard during high school.

We burst from the surface, gasping for air. Layla was awake now, and her normally scarily calm expression was replaced by one of absolute terror. "Eda," she choked out, her chest heaving.

"Can you tread water?" I asked her.

She nodded, gulping oxygen.

"Start doing that. I'll look for some driftwood that we can hang onto." I swam off and found a sturdy piece of wood from the broken boat that was big enough for several people to hang onto.

I brought the wood back to Layla, and she gratefully wrapped her arms around it. "Stay here," I told her. "I've got to find Uncle Pac-Man."

"Do what you gotta do, girl," Layla managed. She gave me a smile.

I swam, looking frantically for my uncle's body. I found him unconscious on a large chunk of the dinghy's hull—it had the words "The Black Pearl" on it. I sighed in relief. He wasn't dead, though his arm looked pretty rough, as it was bent in an unnatural position and had been scraped bloody.

I towed Pac-Man back to Layla and eased him onto our piece of driftwood. Another colossal wave was coming in, and we all held our breaths and held on tightly as it crashed over us.

FWWOOM!

This wave hurled us deep into the water, pummeling our already-bruised-and-battered bodies. Remembering my oxygen T, I shoved it into my mouth and immediately began sucking on the fresh oxygen. I gestured to Layla to put hers in her mouth as well, and she grabbed it and started breathing again.

With one hand, I fished around in Pac-Man's pockets for his own oxygen T.

It was gone.

I realized in horror that his oxygen T must've fallen out of his pocket. I groped for my oxygen T and put it in his mouth, never mind the fact that it was coated in my saliva and, therefore, my germs.

Come on, I thought to myself. *Please work. Please don't already have drowned. I really don't want a dead body on my hands.*

To my immense relief, Pac-Man's chest started rising and falling. I mentally sighed and then remembered that I needed to breathe, too. I took the oxygen T out of his mouth, inhaled, and quickly put it back in.

The driftwood rose to the surface, bringing us with it, and as we broke the water, I saw the most magnificent sight ever: the captain's old excuse for a cruise ship.

"CAPTAIN WHATEVER-YOUR-NAME-IS!" I hollered, desperately waving my arms around. "HEY! HELP!"

"SAY, YOU FOLKS NEED A HAND DOWN THERE?" the captain's gravelly, maddeningly cheerful voice boomed via the ship's ancient loudspeaker.

"YES, PLEASE!" Layla yelled.

"ALRIGHTY, I'M THROWIN' THE ANCHOR DOWN TO YE!" the captain thundered. "OH, WAIT, I DON'T HAVE AN ANCHOR. SORRY. HANG ON; I'LL THROW YE A ROPE OR SUP'M!"

A moment later, the captain tossed us a rope that was fortunately long enough to reach the water. I climbed on with Pac-Man, my arm wrapped around his waist so I could carry him (which wasn't easy since the dude, although thin, weighed more than I had expected). Layla clutched at the rope as the captain slowly pulled us up. As he worked, I heard him singing an old children's song: "The Farmer in the Dell."

The captain was halfway through the sixth time singing the song when we finally collapsed onto the ship's deck, coughing and sputtering. My eyes stung from the salt water, and after barfing up about a gallon of seawater, I sat up on the deck, which was slick with water.

"Hey, there," said the captain as he recoiled the rope.

I coughed some more. "Thank you."

"Oh, don't mention it," the captain said. "'Twas my pleasure."

I crawled over to where Pac-Man lay, his arm hanging at a funny angle, and checked on him. "Uncle?" I whispered.

Pac-Man's eyes fluttered open. "Eda?"

"Don't move," I commanded him. "I think your arm is broken." I started looking for a first aid kit. Behind me, I heard Pac-Man yelp in agony.

"Yup, it's definitely broken," Pac-Man squeaked.

"I *said*, don't move." I finally located a first aid kit and did my best to bandage his arm and make him a sling. He hissed in pain as I dabbed alcohol on his cuts and scrapes and then wrapped his arm with a clean, dry cloth.

"You know, it hasn't been three days yet, but after I left you kiddies out here, I got a bad feeling in these bones of mine," the captain said as he turned the boat around, "so I came back to check on ye. And lo and behold, you're capsized in the ocean with waves beatin' ye black an' blue, and you've destroyed my favorite (and only) dinghy! So, of course, I rescued you. Now you owe me twice as much as ye originally did, as you damaged my dinghy beyond repair."

I sighed and sat down. "I know."

After I checked on Layla to make sure she was okay, I joined the captain at the helm. The sky began to clear, and the ocean calmed as we sailed back to Florida.

Naturally, as soon as the hospital in Daytona released Pac-Man and we were able to go back home, my parents freaked out upon seeing the state we were in: Pac-Man, with an arm broken in three different places; me, with several nasty-looking scrapes and a black eye; and Layla, looking totally fine except for a large bruise on her shin. After they had calmed down somewhat, my parents said we were to go to our rooms to reflect on the danger we had just put ourselves through until Frances called for dinner.

We did not exactly do that.

Pac-Man sat on his bed and held his bright-pink cast up to his light for all to see (cue the angelic vocals). "It's only been a day, and already my cast has been signed at least fifty-six times."

"Seamus's signatures make up half of those fifty-six times," Layla said.

"True," said Pac-Man, admiring his cast.

I went to the mini-fridge and got out four Sprites. "Here we all are," I said, passing one to Layla, Pac-Man, and Alfie.

"Thanks, child," said Alfie. An invisible hand reached out and grabbed the Sprite.

"You're welcome, Alfie," I said.

"You know what?" said Alfie, popping the tab.

"What?" we said in unison.

"We should have a toast. Romans had toasts all the time. It was a bit of a tradition to have a toast at every feast or party. And your homecoming should be celebrated, I think." Alfie sipped the Sprite.

"Yeah, we should do that," said Layla. She raised her Sprite and declared, "A toast to our inevitable, but hopefully very late, deaths!"

"A toast to our inevitable, but hopefully very late, deaths!" we echoed. We all raised our sodas to our lips and drank.

EPILOGUE

Cassidy Weldon

The Ghost Realm is back to normal. Harry Houdini has fixed what he started, and my bungalow has been restored (hooray!). O'Riley's Pizzeria is back in business (also hooray), and Carrie Nation has been put in an alcohol-free neighborhood. I remain in contact with Eda, and she has continued her visits every five years now that the Realm is stable again. Stroopwafels are never absent from my refrigerator. Greg has a passion for chickens, ever since I forced through the rule change on animals, so we got some and built a coop in the backyard. And Theodore Humphrey, the old Devil, resigned from his position to achieve his long-time dream of becoming a quarterback for Hell's football team, and now Houdini has replaced him as the Devil.

In short, death is good in the Ghost Realm.

One day, I come home from work to find Eda lounging on

my couch on a surprise visit. I drop my bags and run over. "Eda! You aren't supposed to be here for another six months!"

"Cass! I couldn't wait," she says, equally excited. We hug, and I step back to take a look at her. She appears just the same as ever, except that she wears a thin silver ring around her middle finger.

"What's that?" I ask, gesturing at the ring.

Eda grins, bouncing up and down on the balls of her feet. "Layla proposed to me. We're engaged now."

I hug her again. "That's great, Eda!"

"Do you want to go swing on the tire?" Eda asks.

I nod. I've missed that.

We run to the balcony, jump off, land perfectly (me landing like a cat, as usual), and take off toward the tire swing. "Last sister there's a rotten egg," I yell and put on a burst of speed.

Eda beats me anyway. I blame her long legs.

"Looks like you're a rotten egg, Cass," she teases as I arrive.

I swat at her arm playfully. "It's not fair! You're the one with the advantage. Next time we do this, I get a ten-second head start."

"Fine," says Eda. She tucks a strand of hair behind her ear. "You want to go first this time?"

"Okay," I say. I clamber onto the tire and take a moment to get settled before Eda seizes the tire. She pushes me back and forth before spinning me around and around and around. She isn't as strong as I am, but she's still really good. I laugh as I twirl around, the wind mussing up my hair.

"Do it again," I say after the tire stops spinning. My sister obliges and proceeds to spin me faster than before.

And suddenly, I'm flying through the air. The moon is out, and I pass by as I soar. I laugh and laugh and laugh and think to myself, *Now* this *is paradise.*

NOTES

CHAPTER 5

1. Kids, don't try this at home, because a coma is very dangerous. You could die.

Made in the USA
Columbia, SC
02 February 2023

11443522R00093